Will Nancy and Ned Work Things Out?

"Ned, please try to understand," Nancy said, annoyed that he was making her feel guilty again. Grabbing a notebook and pen from her desk, she shoved them into her shoulder bag, along with her mini tape recorder.

"It's okay. Don't worry about me," Ned finally said. Nancy didn't get the feeling that he meant it, but at least he was trying.

"This shouldn't take more than an hour," she told him, throwing the bag over her shoulder and heading for the door. She stopped with her hand on the knob.

"Ned, I'm sorry. I really am," she said, glancing back at him. "But I have to do this. We still have the rest of the weekend to talk."

Ned gave her a long, sober look. Then he shrugged and said, "Okay." But Nancy could tell that she'd let him down—again.

Nancy Drew on Campus™

#1 New Lives, New Loves
#2 On Her Own

Available from ARCHWAY Paperbacks

Nancy Drew
on campus™ #2

On Her
Own

Carolyn Keene

AN ARCHWAY PAPERBACK
Published by POCKET BOOKS
New York London Toronto Sydney Tokyo Singapore

AN ARCHWAY PAPERBACK *Original*

An Archway Paperback published by
POCKET BOOKS, a division of Simon & Schuster Inc.
1230 Avenue of the Americas, New York, NY 10020

Copyright © 1995 by Simon & Schuster Inc.
Produced by Mega-Books, Inc.

ISBN: 0-671-52741-X

First Archway Paperback printing October 1995

10 9 8 7 6 5 4 3 2 1

NANCY DREW, AN ARCHWAY PAPERBACK and colophon are registered trademarks of Simon & Schuster Inc.

NANCY DREW ON CAMPUS is a trademark of Simon & Schuster Inc.

Cover photos by Pat Hill Studio

Printed in the U.S.A.

IL 8+

On Her
Own

CHAPTER 1

"I'm lucky I found you," Nancy Drew called out to her two best friends, Bess Marvin and George Fayne. "I had no idea this would be such a mob scene."

"Welcome to Friday afternoon of Rush Week," George said with a grin, glancing at the waves of girls that were sweeping in and out of the Victorian houses on Wilder University's Sorority Row. "It's total chaos!"

"Actually, Rush Week doesn't officially start until next week," Bess explained. "This is more like an open house. We can tour the sororities and get a feel for which ones we like before we pick the ones to rush." Her blue eyes danced with excitement as she glanced at the different houses. "Isn't it great?"

Nancy wasn't sure the sorority scene was for her, but she couldn't help getting caught up in Bess's enthusiasm. "It's worth checking out, anyway," she said.

"Not everyone is as enthusiastic about sororities as you are, Bess," George added. "For some of us, college isn't *just* a social scene."

"I didn't hear that. Not from my own cousin." Bess clamped her hands over her ears, looking horrified. "You obviously don't have your priorities straight."

Nancy had to laugh. Although Bess and George were related, they were complete opposites. Bess's mind was usually focused on partying and cute guys, while George's mind was intent on more serious and down-to-earth matters, such as academics and sports. They even looked different. George was tall, with wavy dark hair and a natural athlete's build. Bess was shorter and more curvy, with long blond hair.

"Priorities, eh?" Nancy echoed. "You sound like Gail Gardeski, the paper's editor-in-chief." She rolled her eyes and let her backpack drop to the ground. "She just spent the last half hour of our editorial meeting lecturing us about how *Wilder Times* should be our biggest priority."

"You do want to be a journalist," George put in.

Nancy nodded. "Sure, but I always pictured myself in exotic foreign places, uncovering stories about spies and traitors."

"I haven't seen too many spies around here, Nan," George cracked. She glanced at Wilder's beautifully landscaped lawns and the ivy-covered brick buildings of the academic quad nearby.

"No kidding," Nancy said. "That must be why

all I've done so far is proofread, get supplies, and rearrange paper clips—all the stuff upperclassmen can't be bothered with."

"Ooooh. Paper clips! Who says journalism's not glamorous?" Bess teased.

"I must be making progress, though," Nancy said. "One of my jobs this week is to get quotes from people at tomorrow's football game. It's for a human-interest piece to show how excited everyone is about our Wilder Norsemen being the number-one team in our conference."

"That should help drum up interest for the game next week against last year's state champs, the Brockton Cougars," George added.

"Exactly," Nancy said, nodding. "Anyway, if I don't screw up my quotes assignment, maybe Gail will give me a shot at doing more important reporting." She ran a hand through her long reddish blond hair, letting out a sigh. "Not that I really have time to work on it this weekend, with Ned coming and everything."

"That's right! I totally forgot he's going to be here," Bess exclaimed. She gave Nancy a sympathetic look. "Serious discussion time?"

"I guess," Nancy answered halfheartedly. "We've talked on the phone about maybe cooling things off, but . . . I don't know. We finally decided that seeing each other in person is the only way we're ever going to figure out what we want to do."

"Maybe once Ned sees how happy you are at Wilder, he'll understand that you were right to come here instead of going to Emerson," George put in.

"That's what I'm hoping." Nancy couldn't put into words right then what was happening between her and Ned. It wasn't just that she'd decided to enroll at a different college from him. It was about their growing and changing and being true to themselves without holding the other person back.

"Stop looking so serious, Nancy," said Bess. "You and Ned always work things out, right?"

Nancy had to take a deep breath before answering. "I have a feeling that if we break up this time, it could be for good."

For a moment Bess wasn't sure she'd heard right. "You and Ned break up? For good?" she asked. "That would be like altering the course of the entire universe."

"*Now* who's being melodramatic?" George said.

"Things are definitely not the same anymore," Nancy admitted. "Starting college has meant a lot of changes for all of us."

Too bad most of my changes have been for the worse, thought Bess.

She envied Nancy and George, who both seemed so happy at Wilder. But then they didn't have a roommate who acted like a drill sergeant. And they hadn't registered too late to get into the drama class they really wanted. Nor did they have a biology class with Professor Ross. Just thinking about him gave her a stomachache.

That wasn't even the worst of it. Bess couldn't go to sleep at night without having nightmares about what had happened at the first frat party she'd gone to at Wilder. Every time she closed her eyes, she pictured Dave Cantera's leering face and the way he'd tried to corner her alone in his room. She knew she'd been lucky to get away.

"Bess!" A guy's voice broke into her thoughts.

She felt her bleak mood melt away as she turned around and saw Brian Daglian, the one new male friend she'd made at Wilder. He jogged toward her, the wind ruffling his blond hair.

"Hi, Brian. Don't tell me you're thinking of joining the track team?" she teased, punching him lightly on the arm.

"Shh. Not so loud," he said in a dramatic stage whisper. "You'll ruin my reputation as a couch potato." He flashed Bess a wide smile, his green eyes sparkling. "Actually, I'm heading into town to look for a black motorcycle jacket and some hair grease. I figured that would help create the right mood when we practice our lines for Monday's audition."

"Good idea," she told him. The drama department at Wilder was holding auditions for *Grease!* Bess didn't think there was much hope of her getting a part, but rehearsing with Brian at least made her forget how dreary the rest of her life had become. "I'll meet you at Hewlitt at seven-thirty," she said, naming the university's theater complex.

"See you then. Bye." Brian gave a quick wave

to the three girls, then breezed left along the path that led into the town of Weston.

Bess turned back to Nancy and George. Pulling a sheet of paper from her bag, she said, "I made a list of all the sororities on campus and marked the ones I thought we might like."

"Too bad you're not this organized when it comes to your classes," George commented.

"Very funny," Bess said, grimacing. She tried not to think about the mixed-up jumble of notes, handouts, and books waiting on her desk back at the dorm. "Anyway, I want to see Theta. I've heard it's a party sorority, but it might be fun. Then there's Tau. Jock City. Not my style, but I thought you might like it, George. Oh, and you'd like this one, too—Pi Phi. I think their members take on environmental causes."

"I think I heard Kara mention that one," Nancy said. Kara Verbeck was Nancy's roommate. "She's rushing, too, and said something about liking Pi Phi because they work to save dolphins and stuff."

"I still don't know if joining a sorority is for me," George said. "I'm afraid that becoming a Tau, or a Pi Phi, or whatever, will isolate me from people who aren't in the sorority. I think I'd rather feel a part of the whole university."

Bess decided not to mention that she didn't feel as if she fit in to any part of Wilder. "I just thought rushing might be fun," she said, shrugging.

"Sure it is." Nancy gave Bess an encouraging

smile. "This one looks nice," she said, pointing to the first house on Sorority Row, a pearl gray Victorian, with white trim and a porch that ran across the front of the first floor.

"You know," Bess said. "Some kids on my floor were talking about a sorority where people are into creative things, like acting and art and dance. They probably wouldn't be interested in me, though," she added quickly.

"Of course not," George said, shaking her head. "Why would they be? You'd only be a natural there."

"You think so?" Bess asked. She was afraid to get too hopeful. After all, nothing at Wilder had turned out the way she'd expected so far.

"Definitely," Nancy told her. "Let's find it. What's it called?"

Bess bit her lip, trying to remember. "I think it starts with a K."

"Kappa?" an unfamiliar voice spoke up.

Bess turned around to see a young woman with warm brown eyes and long, wavy golden hair. She was wearing blue- and black-checked leggings and a blue T-shirt.

"That's it!" Bess exclaimed, smiling back. "Do you know the sorority?"

"I should hope so. I'm their vice president, Holly Thornton," the girl said. She shifted an armful of books to her left arm and held out her right hand. "But I spend so much time over at the theater complex that some of my sorority sisters wonder if I really exist."

"You're into drama?" Bess asked excitedly.

"Set design, actually. I've been working on the sets for *Grease!*"

"You're kidding. I'm trying out for the chorus next week," Bess said, her words tumbling out. "Oh! I'm Bess Marvin, by the way. And this is George Fayne and Nancy Drew."

"Nice to meet you. Kappa's right here," Holly said, pointing to the gray house Nancy had commented on. "Why don't you come in and meet everyone?"

Bess started toward the house, then stopped when she realized that Nancy hadn't moved. She was looking at her watch and frowning. "Don't you want to go in?" Bess asked her.

"I didn't realize how late it was. I should get back to my dorm. Ned's going to be here really soon," Nancy said apologetically.

"And I have to go check the schedule for crew team," George added. "It's all the way down at the boathouse. I want to get over there and take a run around the lake before it gets dark."

"Oh," Bess said, frowning slightly.

What did you think? she asked herself. That sorority rushes would suddenly make Nancy and George want to spend all their time with you, the way they used to?

As soon as the thought came to her, Bess realized that that was exactly what she had been hoping. But things were different now. She had to make her own life at Wilder.

"Are you coming, Bess?" Holly asked.

She smiled and started toward the house. "Sure. Let's go."

George felt the cool autumn air fill her lungs as she breathed in deeply, finding her stride. The lake and boathouse were nestled into the woods behind the campus. George ran on the gravel drive that wound down past the trees toward the water. The low afternoon sun set the autumn leaves into a blaze of yellows, oranges, greens, and reds.

She felt a little guilty about leaving Bess alone at Sorority Row, but the more she thought about rushing, the less she thought she was interested. Anyway, now that they'd been here for a couple weeks, Bess seemed to be getting used to Wilder.

George felt lucky that most things had been going smoothly for her. Pam Miller was a really cool roommate, her classes were great—and as for guys...

She smiled to herself, picturing Will Blackfeather's strong, angular face and shining black eyes. So far they were just friends, but there was definitely something brewing.

Up ahead, George heard the rhythmic thumping of another runner making steady progress toward her. When the person came into view, George blinked in surprise. "Hey! I was just thinking about you," she said automatically.

Will was wearing a sweat-stained T-shirt and running shorts. A red bandanna was tied around his forehead to keep his dark hair out of his face.

When he saw her, Will's whole face lit up, and George felt a surge of adrenaline that didn't have anything to do with running.

"Hey, yourself," he said, slowing to a stop in front of her. His dark eyes were shining with the warmest, most amazing glow George had ever seen. "So, have you heard anything new from the Selective Service, *Mr.* Fayne?" he asked, grinning at her.

"Not since they froze my bank account," George answered with a groan. "My parents keep sending me money, but I haven't been able to straighten things out. Every time I call, either I get put on hold, or I end up talking to some jerk who refuses to believe that George Fayne is a girl."

George grimaced as she thought about the bureaucratic screwup that had the Selective Service thinking she was a guy who had failed to register for the draft. Trying to set things right was turning out to be a huge pain. The phones in her dorm hadn't been turned on until a week into the semester, so she had to make endless, frustrating calls from the campus pay phones. There was a silver lining to the whole mess because it was at one of those pay phones that she'd met Will. He'd offered to let her call from his apartment.

"Thanks for letting me use your phone that day," George went on. "You know you took a serious risk, associating with a hardened criminal like me."

Will gave her a teasing grin. "Maybe I like to live dangerously."

"You can't say I didn't warn you," George said, laughing. She started to jog in place. "Well, I should keep running," she said reluctantly.

"Yeah. Me, too." Will took a step past George, then paused to look back at her. "Are you doing anything tomorrow night?" he asked.

George felt an electric current buzz through her. "Not really," she told him. "Why?"

"Even hardened criminals have to eat," Will said. "I thought we could have dinner and maybe see a movie or something?" He said it casually, but George didn't miss the gleam in his eyes.

Grinning at him, she said, "You've got a deal."

George was still glowing as she ran down the hill to the dirt parking lot next to the boathouse. The low wooden building stretched along the lake, with a dock running the length of it. Inside, George passed by crew shells, canoes, sailboats, and rowboats as she headed for the bulletin board, which was covered with sign-up sheets and information.

A girl with brown hair was standing there. When George saw her freckled face and square build, she recognized her immediately.

"You're Eileen, right? One of Nancy Drew's suitemates?" George asked. Seeing the girl's surprised expression, she quickly added, "I'm her friend George. I live in Jamison Hall, but we met when Nancy first moved into Thayer."

11

"Right," Eileen said. "You guys are from the same town. River Heights, right?" She grinned at George, then pointed to a typed list tacked to the bulletin board. "I guess we're going to be seeing a lot of each other. We're in the same shell."

"Cool," George said. She glanced at the six other names but didn't recognize any of them. "We start practice Monday morning, huh?" she said, pointing to the schedule next to the list.

"At six sharp," Eileen said, groaning. "This is going to put a serious damper on my partying schedule. I'll just have to make up for it by going all out this weekend."

George laughed, following Eileen as she left the boathouse. "Is there anything special going on?" George asked.

"Are you kidding? If we win tomorrow's game, the Beta fraternity is throwing a huge party. Practically the whole football team lives there, so you know there'll be tons of gorgeous guys. And—"

Eileen suddenly stopped talking. Her gaze was fixed on a group of guys in running gear who had just come into the parking lot. "Talk about gorgeous," Eileen said under her breath. "That's Scott Berenson!"

"The quarterback?" George gave the four guys a closer look. They all had muscular builds and were shoving one another and clowning around. "Everyone calls him Scooter, right? Which one is he?"

"Cut-off sweats, dark hair, and blinking neon

sign over his head that says 'Most Gifted and Gorgeous Guy on the Planet,'" Eileen said dreamily. "Don't look now, but he's headed our way."

The guys stopped a few feet from them and started to do cooling-down stretches. George wasn't sure if she was imagining things, but Scooter seemed to be giving her a lot of sideways glances.

Eileen jabbed George in the ribs with her elbow, then called out to the guys. "Hey! Good luck for tomorrow's game. Not that you'll need it, of course."

"You got that right," a guy with curly blond hair said. "People have a lot riding on the game. They know we're not going to let 'em down." He gave Scooter a high five. "We're going to slam the Chargers into the ground, right, Scooter?"

Scooter nodded, then sauntered closer to George and Eileen. "Definitely," he said, his eyes flicking over George. "Did we ever meet before?" he asked her.

George shook her head. "I don't think so." She couldn't believe it when he gave her a killer smile a second later. Scooter Berenson was actually flirting with her!

"Too bad," he went on. "Why don't you come to our party tomorrow night?"

George wasn't sure what to say, but when Eileen elbowed her in the ribs, she mumbled, "Sure. Maybe."

"Cool." Scooter wiped his forehead with his wristband, then asked, "Do you live in Tau?"

"No, she's in Jamison Hall," Eileen put in quickly.

"I'll pick you up at seven-thirty." Scooter shot George another smile, then headed up the drive with his teammates. "See you then. Oh, by the way, what's your name?"

"George Fayne." It took George a second after they disappeared to realize what had just happened. "I thought he was just inviting us," she said slowly. "I didn't know it was, like, a date."

"You are *sooo* lucky," Eileen said. But George barely heard her.

"I'm a total idiot!" she groaned. "I can't go out with Scooter Berenson."

"What?" Eileen was staring at George as if she'd just said she was from another planet. "Why not?"

"I know he's the star of the football team, but I already have a date for tomorrow night, with a guy named Will," George explained. She looked helplessly at Eileen. "What am I going to do?"

CHAPTER 2

"Scooter, wait!" George started to run to catch up with the quarterback, but Eileen grabbed her arm.

"Are you nuts?" Eileen whispered. She pulled George back against the boathouse wall. "You can't break a date with Scooter."

"Why not? I just told you, I already have a date," George told her. "I shouldn't have said yes in the first place."

Eileen studied George as if she had suddenly started speaking a foreign language. "I don't know if you totally understand what just happened. *Scooter Berenson* asked you out. Need I say more?"

"I guess I'm flattered," George said slowly, "but I can't—"

"George," Eileen interrupted. "Girls worship the ground he walks on. If you don't go to that party with him tomorrow night, there are plenty of other girls at Wilder who'll fight to take your place. You might not get a second chance." Eileen gave a dismissive wave. "We've only been here a few weeks. How important could this other guy be to you?"

"His name's Will," George said, suddenly defensive. "Will Blackfeather. I don't feel right about breaking a date, that's all."

It was the truth, but Eileen didn't seem to buy it. She raised an eyebrow at George, a serious expression on her freckled face. "Do what you want, but if you break a date with Scott Berenson, you could regret it for the rest of your life."

Bess bit into a chocolate hazelnut cookie and took in the Kappas' living room. According to Holly, some of the Kappas who were art majors had sponge-painted the walls a soft, warm blend of lemon and apricot. The furniture was a comfortable mix of different styles all soft and overstuffed.

Bess had to pinch herself. Is it really me sitting here? Talking, laughing, having fun? Have I actually found a place at Wilder where I fit in?

She'd already spoken to three drama majors who were going to be working on *Grease!* They'd all seemed pleased that she was auditioning. The other girls she'd met had been really nice, too. Not stuck-up. She hadn't seen a single unpleasant face.

Whoops! Strike that.

Bess's smile faded as she spotted Holly talking

with another girl who kept shooting unfriendly glances at Bess. Holly seemed a little tense.

Bess automatically checked her slacks and flowered T-shirt. Nope, no food stains. So what was the problem? She braced herself as Holly and the other girl made their way over to her.

"Bess, you haven't met Soozie Beckerman yet," Holly said with a forced smile. "She's the secretary of Kappa."

"Nice to meet you," Bess said a little nervously.

Soozie's handshake was clammy and weak, a dead fish in Bess's grasp. She had a phony smile to match. "Holly can't say enough great things about you," Soozie said with no warmth.

That was good, right? Then, why was Soozie studying her so critically?

"Kappa seems like a great place," Bess said. It seemed the safest comment to make.

"It can be," Soozie said. "As long as you don't forget who the really important people are around here." She squinted hard at Bess, then turned away. "Well, see you around. I guess."

I guess? What did that mean? "Did I miss part of the conversation?" Bess asked Holly. "Like maybe the part where I said something really insulting to make her hate me?"

"You didn't do anything. If Soozie's got a problem with anyone around here, it's with me," Holly said. "Don't let her bother you. And don't let her keep you from rushing here." She lowered her voice before adding, "Just between us, a couple of the other Kappas have already told me how much they like you."

Bess felt a warm glow spread through her. "Really? Because I definitely think Kappa is great."

"Not to put any pressure on you, though," Holly said. "After you check out the other sororities, try to make sure Kappa is one you want to rush. What other ones are you considering?"

Bess searched her mind, then listed a few from memory.

"Theta, huh?" Holly said, frowning. "Well, I guess if you're into partying till you drop and drugs and stuff."

"Drugs?" Bess echoed.

Holly nodded. "Theta's the sister sorority to Zeta, where that girl overdosed the first week of the semester."

"Oh. Then forget it," Bess said. She didn't want Holly to think she was a burnout or anything. "I'm already a food junkie," she joked, reaching for another cookie from the tray on the table. "One substance abuse is enough for me, thanks."

"I hear you," Holly said with a laugh. "Anyway, we're having two more open houses this weekend, before all the rush parties next week. It might be a good idea to come to another open house, so more Kappas could meet you. I'd love to see you be invited to pledge here. I hope you'll come."

Bell grinned from ear to ear. "I'll be here."

* * *

"Enough procrastinating," Nancy murmured under her breath. She paused outside the student bookstore and checked her watch. Five-thirty. Ned would be showing up at her dorm, Thayer Hall, any minute now, and she wasn't even there.

She had intended to go straight back to her suite from Sorority Row so she could shower and change into something a little special—at least put on the locket he'd given her.

Then she remembered that she needed a new book for her journalism class and two Wilder T-shirts to send home to her dad and their housekeeper, Hannah Gruen. It wasn't until after she'd paid that she realized she hadn't gotten anything for Ned, which meant going back and picking up a sweatshirt for him.

And now she was late.

"So, why aren't I hurrying?" Nancy wondered out loud.

She took the path that led to her dormitory and breathed a sigh of relief when the modern brick building came into sight a few minutes later. There was no Ned waiting out front. Maybe she'd have time to shower and change after all.

She ran up the steps past the brass columns at the entrance and through the huge glass doors. Inside, the tiled foyer was loud with activity. Some students were checking their mailboxes, others were talking, reading notices on the bulletin boards, or waiting in front of the bank of silver-metal elevators. Since she was only going to the third floor, Nancy decided to take the stairs.

"Nancy?"

The deep, familiar voice made her whirl around. "Ned!"

He was leaning against the wall next to one of the bulletin boards, wearing jeans and a striped shirt with a sweater knotted around his neck. She shouldn't have been surprised at how happy she was to see him, but she was. One look at his handsome, angular face and she completely forgot about how tense and awkward things between them had been lately. She raced across the foyer and threw herself into his arms.

"It's been a long time," Ned whispered, catching her up in a huge hug. "I missed you."

Nancy wasn't sure what to answer. Everything about him was so familiar—the way he smelled, the strength of his arms around her. But had she really missed him?

She was about to step back to look into his face, but stopped herself when she found herself staring into a pair of intense dark eyes. Peter Goodwin. She'd met him only a few times, but they were enough to know that he was smart, funny, and very handsome. He stared hard at her before pushing through the door to the stairs.

Nancy stiffened, suddenly uncomfortable.

"Nan?" Ned's voice was tentative. When she looked into his brown eyes, she was overwhelmed by his concern. "Are you all right?"

"Yeah, fine," she said quickly. She wanted to say more, but what? What was the right thing to say when your whole world was changing and you didn't know where you'd end up? Glancing uneasily around the crowded lobby, she shrugged and said, "Let's go upstairs, okay?"

Ned was quiet as they went up the stairs to the third floor. When they got to Suite 301, they heard music blaring from Liz and Ginny's room, but the lounge was empty. Nancy slowly pushed open the door to her room, then breathed a sigh of relief. Good. Kara wasn't there. Things were delicate enough between her and Ned without a roommate to complicate them.

"Not bad," Ned commented, glancing at the two beds, desks, and dressers.

It was the first positive thing he'd said about Wilder. Maybe George had been right about Ned's coming around once he saw for himself how happy she was at school. "The whole university is great," she said brightly. "I'll give you a tour later, and—"

"I didn't drive three and a half hours to look at scenery and buildings," Ned interrupted gently. He dropped his backpack to the floor and faced Nancy. "We have to talk."

This is it, she thought. After dropping her stuff on her desk, she sat down on the bed. "I know," she said. There was so much to talk about, so much at stake. She wasn't sure where to start. "I want us both to be happy, Ned."

"You think I don't want that, too?" he asked. "I just don't know if we can be happy and stay together." He took a deep breath to calm himself. "You've been pretty distant lately."

Nancy saw his eyes focus on something on her dresser top. Her locket. The one she'd promised never to take off. Seeing the hurt on his face, she felt great sadness. "Look, Ned, I—"

The jangling telephone on her desk made her jump about a foot and a half. This was the last thing they needed! Before it could ring again, she grabbed it.

"Hello?" she said, not bothering to hide her irritation.

"Nancy, is that you? Is something wrong?"

Nancy recognized Gail Gardeski's no-nonsense voice. It was the first time the editor-in-chief had called her. "Hi, Gail. Everything's fine," she lied, not meeting Ned's eyes. "What's up?"

"We've got a problem," Gail told her. "Gary Friedman just called in sick. He was supposed to interview Scott Berenson this afternoon, but he's come down with the flu. I haven't been able to get hold of any of the senior reporters so I need you to get over to the sports complex right away."

"You're kidding!" Nancy felt a surge of excitement. This was exactly the break she'd been waiting for.

"Keep your questions simple," Gail went on. "Ask how he feels about the Norsemen's performance so far, what his predictions are for the game tomorrow and for the one next week with Brockton, what he thinks of his personal performance this season, that kind of thing."

"I could ask about his lucky rabbit's foot, too,"

Nancy put in. "Doesn't he say that's one of the reasons he's doing so well?"

"Mmm," Gail said, but she sounded worried. "I want your article on my desk tomorrow morning. That'll give us time for rewrites."

Gail obviously wasn't thrilled at the idea of a freshman doing such an important interview, but Nancy wasn't going to let that get her down. "I'll take care of it," she promised.

Her mind was racing as she hung up the phone. She'd have to jot down questions on her way to the sports complex.

"What was that all about?" Ned asked.

Nancy blinked in surprise. She'd gotten so caught up in the assignment that she'd totally forgotten that he was there. "That was the editor-in-chief of the school newspaper," she said, trying to keep her voice light. "You're not going to believe this, but I have to do an interview now."

"Now?" Ned said in disbelief.

"I know it's bad timing," she said, "but I don't have any choice. Saying no would be like saying that I'm not serious about the paper, and you know that's not true. Journalism is really important to me."

"A lot more important than *I* am, apparently," he muttered.

"Ned, please try to understand," Nancy said, annoyed that he was making her feel guilty again. Grabbing a notebook and pen from her desk, she shoved them into her shoulder bag, along with her mini tape recorder.

"It's okay. Don't worry about me," Ned finally said. Nancy didn't get the feeling that he meant it, but at least he was trying.

"This shouldn't take more than an hour," she told him, throwing the bag over her shoulder and heading for the door. She stopped with her hand on the knob.

"Ned, I'm sorry. I really am," she said, glancing back at him. "But I have to do this. We still have the rest of the weekend to talk."

Ned gave her a long, sober look. Then he shrugged and said, "Okay." But Nancy could tell that she'd let him down—again.

Ned had paced around Nancy's room half a dozen times before he realized what he was doing. It wasn't until he caught his reflection in the mirror over Nancy's dresser, that he finally stopped.

"Visiting College Student Goes Berserk After Girlfriend Deserts Him," he said to the disgruntled face that stared back at him. "That's going to be Nancy's next article, if we don't talk soon."

He'd been hoping that seeing Nancy face-to-face would somehow make everything right between them—the way it used to be. That all the ways she'd hurt and angered him lately would be wiped away. But then she'd run out on him practically before they'd had a chance to say hello. It brought back all his mixed feelings about her.

"Why did I even bother to come here?" he

groaned, sitting on her bed and dropping his head into his hands.

Deep down, he did know why. He'd been crazy about Nancy for a long time. Sure, they'd grown apart a few times, but they had always found each other again. It was as if there was some law of nature that meant for them to be together.

So what happened?

Face it, he told himself. If she really cared about you, she'd be at Emerson College right now instead of here at Wilder.

It was exactly the kind of thing he'd promised himself not to think, but how could he help it, when Nancy seemed to be pulling further and further away from him with every second?

Is it just her? asked a tiny voice in the back of his mind. Or are *you* pulling away, too?

It was a question he couldn't begin to answer.

Ned's growling stomach reminded him that he hadn't eaten anything since he'd left Emerson. "So much for love feeding hunger," he said out loud. "There must be vending machines around here somewhere."

He strode down the hall to the suite lounge and opened the refrigerator. It was practically empty. "A guy could starve around here," he muttered, closing the door again.

"Obviously you haven't been looking in the right places." A sultry female voice spoke up behind Ned.

He straightened up and glanced back over his shoulder. An attractive girl was standing at the entrance to the lounge. The scoop neck of her light sweater had fallen casually off one shoulder, revealing the strap of a white tank top against her tanned skin. With her high cheekbones, scarlet lipstick, and black hair, she was very dramatic looking. And the expression in her dark eyes revealed that she was frankly appraising Ned.

"Excuse me?" Ned asked.

"You must not be spending time with the right people," the girl went on. "A truly resourceful girl would find a way to satisfy your appetite." She held out her hand to Ned. "I'm Stephanie Keats."

Her body language told Ned that she wasn't just talking about food. This girl was a flirt, and he couldn't help feeling just a little excited. At least someone was paying attention to him.

"I'm Ned Nickerson," he said, and flashed her a smile as he shook her hand. "You were saying?"

Stephanie didn't miss the spark of interest in Ned's eyes. She would have expected Nancy to go out with someone who was a little more forgettable. This guy was a total knockout! And judging by the way he was picking up on her signals, he liked to live a little dangerously. Or maybe he was flirting because there was trouble on the romantic front?

"Ned, huh?" Stephanie pressed her lips together, as if she couldn't quite remember who he was. "I'm sure we've spoken on the phone. Do you know someone in our suite?"

"Nancy Drew," Ned said, frowning. "She's my girlfriend. She must have mentioned me."

He was even sexier when his expression was serious. Hmm, Stephanie thought. This could get interesting. "Not that I can remember," she lied. She gave a breezy wave of her hand. "But with Nancy, it's kind of hard to keep track."

She felt a surge of triumph when she saw Ned's frown deepen. "What do you mean?" he asked.

"I really admire couples who can have an open relationship like yours," Stephanie went on, ignoring his question. "It's great that you can be so understanding about the other guys in her life."

Her words had the exact effect she'd hoped for. Ned's face was burning with anger, his jaw clenched so tight that Stephanie didn't think he'd be able to speak. Perfect! "Where is Nancy, anyway?" Stephanie asked.

Ned mumbled something about an interview, but Stephanie could tell she'd planted a seed of doubt in his mind. How did that saying go? All's fair in love and war? This was definitely war.

"Never mind. I'd like to talk about anything but Wilder for a change," she told him, giving a bored wave. She sat down on the couch and patted the spot next to her. "So, Ned, tell me about yourself."

Footsteps echoed in the empty locker room. They scuffled up the first row of lockers and stopped near the end. It didn't take long to find the right locker. Day-Glo letters spelled out the name—SCOOTER.

Scooter and the rest of the team would be back from their training run in a few minutes. *By then I'll be long gone.*

This was to be the last trip to Scooter's locker. The first had been to set out the details of the plan. Then the second to leave the note "suggesting" that the quarterback play along. And now a request for Scooter's answer.

The note was short and to the point: "This is your chance to team up and score big money. If you agree to go along with the plan, get hold of a ball after Wilder's first TD in tomorrow's game and spike it."

If Scooter didn't agree—well, then, not even his famous rabbit's foot would keep his luck from running out.

The locker room stank of sweat and old socks. When Scooter saw the note, a new scent would be added.

The smell of fear.

CHAPTER 3

Nancy paused at the entrance to the men's locker room. The state-of-the-art sports complex, with a pool, running track, tennis courts, and gym, rose six stories. Behind, a grassy path led to the football field and bleachers. Nancy had been in the women's locker room. But the men's? This was definitely a first.

She stepped to the side as three sweat-soaked guys jogged past, their hair plastered to their foreheads. They gave her sideways glances before heading into the locker room.

"Here goes." Taking a deep breath, she stepped inside the doorway and called out, "Hello! Is Scooter Berenson in here?"

A guy wearing just a towel came to the doorway. "Well, hello," he said, grinning at her. "Hey, Scooter! Looks like there's a special delivery here for you," he called into the locker room. "Very special," he added with a chuckle.

Nancy could feel her cheeks turn bright red. "I'm here to interview Scooter for *Wilder Times,*" she said, trying to keep her cool. "Could you ask him to come out here after he's—"

"Decent?" the guy with the towel finished. "Scooter's never been decent in his life."

"Besides, the tradition around here is for the newspaper to interview us inside the locker room," he told Nancy, giving her a look that was openly challenging. "If you want your story, you'll have to come on in and get it."

Nancy was sure her face would ignite if it got any redder, but she couldn't back down. Her whole future at the paper depended on this assignment. "Fine," she said.

Squaring her shoulders, she strode into the room. The second she entered, whistles and catcalls echoed all around her. Don't look any lower than their chins! she ordered herself. But she couldn't help noticing flashes of bare torsos and skimpy white towels wrapped around players' waists. She could hear showers somewhere to her right.

She didn't know how she made it down the row of lockers, but finally she found Scooter's name on an open locker door. A small rabbit's foot hung on a chain inside. The fur was bright red, obviously dyed. A guy with dark hair was standing in front of the door with his back to her. At least he wasn't half naked, Nancy thought with relief.

"Excuse me. Are you Scooter?"

When he didn't turn around, Nancy stepped around so she could see him. "Scooter? I'm Nancy Drew, a reporter for . . . Scooter, are you all right?"

Scooter Berenson was staring at a piece of paper, not moving. Nancy detected a glimmer of fear in his eyes. Finally he blinked, then did a double take when he saw Nancy. "What? Yeah, I'm fine." He quickly balled the paper up and tossed it into his locker, then angrily asked, "What are you doing in here? This is the men's locker room, in case you hadn't noticed."

Scooter obviously hadn't heard any of his teammates' comments, even though Nancy was sure he'd been within hearing distance. What was on that piece of paper that had kept him so preoccupied and fearful?

"I'm here to interview you for *Wilder Times,*" she explained. Nodding casually at the crumpled up paper in his locker, she added, "Whatever you were reading must have been pretty important."

There it was again, that fearful look. But in a flash it was replaced by a scowl. "You reporters should know when to mind your own business."

Something was wrong, Nancy was sure of it. She opened her mouth to probe more, then stopped. You're here to do an interview, not chase after a mystery, she reminded herself.

"Sorry," she said. She pulled out her minirecorder and turned it on, then glanced at the questions she'd written down. "So, tell me about your famous rabbit's foot," she said, nodding at the lump of red fur. "Is that really what's responsible for your outstanding abilities?"

Scooter seemed to relax a little as he grabbed the chain and fingered the fur. "My high school coach gave this to me after we made state champs two years in a row," he said. "I've never played a game without it."

He was warming up now, his nervousness gone. Maybe what he'd been reading wasn't that big a deal after all.

"What hurricane ripped through here?" George asked as she stepped into Jamison Hall's fourth-floor laundry room. Her roommate, Pam Miller, was kneeling on the floor next to a pile of tangled clothes. Pam's dark, burnished skin and long, straight black hair glowed under the room's fluorescent lights.

"I'm not sure, but this is a national emergency, no doubt about it," Pam said. Sitting back on her heels, she grinned at George and held up an assortment of socks twisted around each other. "We're going to have to launch a massive cleanup effort if I'm ever going to find my yellow shirt. I knew I shouldn't have left my stuff in the washer when I went to class this afternoon."

George started poking at a pile of wet things on the floor next to the door. "Is this it?" she asked, holding up a wrinkled yellow bundle she'd pulled from the pile.

"My shirt! Thanks." Pam took it from her, and

gathering up the rest of her clothes, put them in an empty dryer.

George told her roommate about her date dilemma. "I'd much rather go out with Will," she finished. "What do you think? Would it be totally crazy to break the date with Scott Berenson?"

"Scooter is an amazing athlete," Pam said over the hum of the dryer. "Even if you don't want to get romantic, it might be cool to see what he's all about. I mean, how often does a sports nut like you or me have the chance to get to know someone who's probably going to be a superstar in the NFL in a few years?"

"I see what you mean," George said. "Maybe I wouldn't exactly have to cancel my date with Will. I might be able to reschedule it for another night."

She waited for her roommate to say something, but Pam was staring off into space. "Pam? Are you all right?"

"Oh—sorry." Pam blinked, then smiled apologetically at George. "I was just thinking, that's all."

"About Jamal?" George guessed. Pam's boyfriend was a sophomore at Wilder. He and Pam had been going out since high school. In fact, Jamal was the main reason Pam had decided to go to Wilder. But George knew that she'd been worried about him lately.

Pam nodded. "He's waiting for me back in our room. If you see someone pacing in there like a caged tiger, don't be alarmed. It's just Jamal."

"He's still tense?" George asked.

"That's way too relaxed a description," she said. "I mean, he's got his classes and a full-time job at Sports World. On top of that, he's rethinking his future. When he hurt his ankle last year, he couldn't play football anymore and lost his football scholarship. I know he needs money for tuition and books and everything, but I wish he'd cut back on his hours at the store. I think he's taken on more than he can handle."

No wonder she's worried, George thought.

"I've tried to talk to him about it," Pam went on, "but he just blows up at me."

When they got back to their room, Jamal was sitting at Pam's desk with an economics book open in front of him. George didn't miss the stiff set of his jaw or the way his right high-top was tapping a mile a minute against the tiled floor.

"Hey, Jamal. How's it going?" George said.

"Not bad," Jamal said with a tense smile. "How's it going for you?"

"George is about to become a famous personality on campus," Pam answered for George. She went over to her boyfriend and playfully tapped his shoulder. "After her date with Scott Berenson tomorrow night, everyone is going to know who she is."

"Scott Berenson?" Jamal's jaw became rigid again. "Don't tell me you're going to play into his ego act, too?"

What was Jamal so mad about? George wondered. It wasn't as if he had to spend time with Scooter.

"Arrogant jerks like him think the world is just waiting to hand them whatever they want," he said bitterly. "I'd like to see that guy suffer, just once. Then he'd see what life is like for the rest of us."

"Chill out," Pam said, shooting George an apologetic glance. "Look, why don't we go outside and get some fresh air."

Jamal caught himself before he said anything else about Scooter and flipped his economics book closed. "Fine," he said. "Later, George."

What's his problem? thought George as she watched the door close behind them. She'd been with Jamal a few times, but he'd never acted quite that uptight. Something was definitely bothering him. She just hoped Pam figured out what it was before it hurt their relationship.

Speaking of relationships, I've got a few things to work out in my own life, she thought. Like deciding who to go out with tomorrow night.

You know that Will means more to you, she told herself, and decided to cancel Scooter.

After picking up the phone, she dialed the campus operator and asked for the number for Zeta. While the phone rang, Pam's words kept coming back to her. How often *would* she get the chance to get to know someone who would probably turn pro?

" 'Lo?" a gruff voice answered.

George slammed down the receiver. She just couldn't do it.

But how could she break her date with Will? What if he got the wrong idea about why she wanted to go out with Scooter?

After taking a deep breath, she looked up Will's number in her book and then dialed it. "Hi, Will. It's George," she said when he answered. "Listen, about tomorrow night, I have some bad news. . . ."

"Yo, Will! What's the matter?"

Hearing his roommate's voice, Will realized he'd been staring blankly at a burn mark on the kitchen counter, below where the phone hung on the wall. He blinked and looked over the counter at Andy Rodriguez, who was sprawled on the couch in the tiny living area of their apartment. Andy's feet were propped up on the wooden crate that served as a coffee table. "Sorry. What did you say?"

"Didn't I hear the words *movie* and *dinner* being tossed around?" Andy asked. "Sounds like you and George are finally going out. So why do you look as if you just flunked midterms?"

Because now another day would pass before he'd have a chance to see George again, was the answer that immediately came to Will's mind. Because he'd wanted to tell her in person what he'd been doing to help solve her problems with the Selective Service.

"We were going to go out tomorrow night, but

something's come up and she can't make it," he told Andy. "We're going out on Sunday instead. It's no big deal."

Andy gave Will a sidelong glance before flicking the TV's remote control. "So I guess she means absolutely nothing to you, right? I mean, she's only pretty, smart, and nice." He gave a dismissive shrug. "Not at all the kind of girl you'd be interested in."

"What do you want me to say?" Will asked, holding up his hands defensively. "That George is a girl I could really fall for?"

"For starters," Andy said with a grin. "Anyway, if you want my opinion, I think she's a huge improvement over Angela."

Will rolled his eyes. "So, I made a mistake. How was I supposed to know Angela was a total airhead?"

"Not to mention that she was dating two other guys at the same time she was seeing you," Andy put in.

"Thanks for reminding me," Will said, grimacing. "Anyway, that was last year. What's going on between George and me is totally different. George doesn't seem like the kind of girl who'd play games."

Kara stared at herself in the mirror over her dresser. She wasn't wearing anything special. Just a cropped shirt and jeans, but they showed off all her curves. She could imagine Vic's reaction when he saw her. Just thinking about it sent a tiny shiver through her.

"Kara Verbeck, you are the luckiest girl at Wilder," she told her reflection. After all, how many freshman girls were going out with a quarterback on the number-one team in the conference? She didn't care that Vic Margolis was second string. He made her feel so amazingly wonderful. He could be the team's water boy and she'd feel the same way about him.

Letting out a dreamy sigh, Kara put on some lipstick, then reached for her bag. She was about to leave, when she spotted the brown leather jacket draped over the back of Nancy's desk chair. "Hey, this looks new," she murmured out loud.

The leather was butter soft, and the cut was sleek and simple. It would look perfect with . . .

In a flash Kara had slipped it on. "Yes!" She smiled at her reflection, turning left and right to take in the different angles.

Nancy wouldn't mind if she borrowed it. They had an understanding about sharing things. And, anyway, Nancy wouldn't be needing it—not when her boyfriend was waiting for her in the lounge. Ned looked as if he was more than capable of keeping her warm.

Smiling to herself, Kara reached for her bag, threw it over the shoulder of Nancy's jacket, and breezed out of the room.

* * *

Why didn't I bring my jacket? Nancy wondered as she turned onto the path that led to Thayer Hall.

The sun had set, and a light evening breeze whipped through her shirt. Nancy picked up her pace, breaking into a jog. She couldn't wait to get inside. But being cold wasn't the only reason she was hurrying.

The interview with Scooter had gone great, but it had lasted longer than she'd anticipated. It was already after seven-thirty. She didn't think Ned was going to appreciate being left alone for so long.

Nancy was about ten feet from the dorm, when she saw Kara come barreling through the doors. "Oh—hi!" she said, hurrying past. She zipped up the leather jacket as she went.

"Hey! Isn't that *my* jacket?" Nancy asked, doing a double take.

"Doesn't it look great on me?" Kara did a quick pirouette, then continued toward the mall, her auburn hair blowing in the wind. "Gotta run. I'm late to meet Vic," she called over her shoulder. "See you."

Nancy felt slightly annoyed. It was starting to get old, the way Kara constantly borrowed her stuff. Oh, well. Don't let it get you down. You've got enough on your mind already.

She ran the rest of the way to the dorm, then took the stairs two at a time to the third floor. "Oh, hi, Liz," she said just outside the door to Suite 301.

Liz Bader shared a room with Ginny Yuen, one of Nancy's suitemates. There was something about the slender New Yorker that Nancy liked, but she hadn't really gotten to know either Liz or Ginny that well yet.

"Hi," Liz answered. "Hey, Ned seems like a nice guy."

"You met him? Great," Nancy said. "I was afraid he'd get bored."

"I don't think you have to worry about that. Stephanie's been keeping him occupied." Liz gave her a look Nancy couldn't quite read, then opened the door to the suite and ducked inside.

Uh-oh, Nancy thought as a peal of laughter floated out from the lounge. It was followed by Stephanie's sultry voice.

"Ned, you are too much," Stephanie was saying. "Nancy must not appreciate what she has, leaving you alone here so long." Her voice lowered an octave, and she added, "Not that I'm complaining."

Nancy felt her hands tighten at her side. What a flirt! Stephanie knew that Ned was her boyfriend, yet she was coming on to him.

"Hey, I'm perfectly happy with the company," Ned said.

Nancy's jaw fell open. I don't believe this! He's actually falling for it!

She hesitated, feeling angry and insecure at the same time. It really hurt to hear that special tone in Ned's voice when he was talking to another girl. What was going on here?

Nancy didn't know the answer to that question yet. But she had the sinking suspicion that things were only going to get worse.

"How's the moo shu pork?"

"Good." Nancy pointed her chopstick at the pork-filled pancake she'd just prepared. "Want some?"

Ned shook his head. "No, thanks."

Nancy sighed to herself as they fell quiet once again. So far, dinner had been filled with uncomfortable silences. Since she'd gotten back from her interview, neither of them had exactly been bubbling with enthusiasm. Finally she couldn't take it anymore.

"Why'd you do it, Ned? Did you have to flirt with Stephanie Keats, of all people?" she asked. She couldn't keep the hurt from her voice. "Our lives are complicated enough already."

At least he had the decency to act embarrassed. But as he poked his fork into his shrimp fried rice, she could see that he was angry, too. "Maybe that's why I did it," Ned told her. "Because I can't figure out where we stand. I feel as if you're a totally different person now. I mean, I used to think you were honest."

Nancy just stared at him. "What's that supposed to mean?"

"It means that if you want to see other guys, you should tell me!" he shot back.

"Other guys?" she echoed. That had come flying out of left field. How could he even think that?

Ned flashed her an angry look. "From what Stephanie told me, you've been getting pretty hot and heavy lately in the dating game."

"And you believed her?" Nancy blinked furiously to keep the tears from filling her eyes. To think that he'd take Stephanie's word over hers. He couldn't possibly know how much that hurt her. "I'd never lie to you, Ned."

Looking across the table, she saw his expression soften. She'd never seen so much pain or sadness in his strong, angular face.

"How am I supposed to know what to believe?" he finally said. "Do you think I'm happy about the way I feel right now? I never thought I'd doubt what we have. I want us to be together. I really do. But not like this. I can't go on feeling as if I'm at the bottom of your list of priorities."

Nancy opened her mouth to tell him once again how busy she was, and how she needed time to get settled and start her life here. Then she stopped herself. She'd only be kidding herself—and lying to Ned.

"I don't know what's happening," she finally admitted, "but I do know I need my independence right now." Seeing his frown, she added quickly, "It's not about other guys, Ned. It's just that I need to make a life here at Wilder. And, well, I don't feel as if I can do that and be with you at the same time."

Ned didn't say anything; he just sat pushing

some rice around on his plate with his fork. It seemed like forever before he finally met her eyes. "So that's it?" he asked. "We're breaking up?"

Nancy glanced around the restaurant, as if someone there could tell her which buttons to push to make things right again between her and Ned. But she knew it wasn't that easy. When she looked back at him, her eyes were filled with tears.

"Yes," she answered. "I guess we are."

CHAPTER 4

Bess took a sip of her cappuccino and looked around Java Joe's, Wilder University's coffee bar. It was Friday night, and the place was packed. "I love hanging out here," she confided to Brian. "It almost makes me feel like a normal college student."

"Normal—you?" Brian laughed. "I don't think so."

"I did say almost," Bess said, giggling. "Anyway, thanks for rehearsing with me for Monday's audition. Not that I stand a chance of getting a part. I know I'm not nearly as good as you are."

"Well, that goes without saying," Brian said. "Just kidding. Come on, Bess, you're a natural. You definitely have what it takes."

Bess wished she could believe him, but she knew the odds were stacked against her. "Freshmen hardly ever get parts," she said.

She waited for him to say something, but he

was staring dreamily at the glossy tabletop. "We'll have to move out of our dorms, you know," he murmured.

"Huh?" Bess was confused as she glanced at him over the top of her cappuccino.

"After the play opens," he went on. "There's just not enough security. Who'll keep our adoring fans at bay?"

He grinned at her, and Bess burst out laughing. "You're crazy! We haven't even auditioned yet."

"Oh, right. Well, anyway, I'm glad we're doing it together," he told her.

That was the understatement of the year. "Are you kidding?" she said. "Without your support I'd fall apart, Brian."

"So you're not going to forget all about me once you're in a sorority and have a whole new set of popular friends?" he asked. He said it jokingly, but something in his voice caught Bess's attention.

"No way would I drop you," she said. "You can't get rid of me *that* easily."

He looked relieved. "I know it sounds weird. It's just that our friendship means a lot to me, that's all."

For once he sounded completely serious. Gazing at him across the table, Bess was struck by an amazing idea. Was Brian flirting with her?

She picked up her cappuccino to hide the blush she felt rising to her cheeks. Don't panic, she ordered herself.

Bess quickly went down a checklist of things

she felt around guys she had crushes on. Goose bumps? Incredible nervousness whenever he's around? Inability to say anything that makes sense when you talk to him?

Bess let out her breath. The answer was no on all counts. In fact, when she was with Brian, she didn't feel any of the giddiness and confusion that came over her when she was around cute guys.

"Earth to Bess. Come in, Bess."

She blinked, then realized that he was staring at her expectantly. "Uh, sorry. What did you say?"

"We're on again for Sunday, right?" he asked. "Same time, same place?"

He was grinning again—that amazing smile that lit up his whole face. "Definitely," she replied.

Mmm, she thought. Maybe feeling this comfortable around a guy is what real love is all about. Maybe the reason I haven't met anyone else yet is because I'm not meant to meet anyone else.

Bess gave a dreamy sigh and stirred her cappuccino. Brian and I might be destined to become more than just friends.

Leslie King tapped her pencil eraser against her chemistry lab report, then checked the glowing digital numbers on her wristwatch. 10:30. "Where *is* he?" she wondered out loud. "He was supposed to be here an hour ago."

Maybe Tom Bowles was one of the most intelligent upperclassmen at Wilder, but apparently being smart didn't make him punctual. It was the kind of thing that drove her crazy. But in Tom's case, she was willing to let it slide.

A sound outside the door made Leslie jump up from her desk chair. "Hi!" she called. "I was beginning to wonder if you'd ever . . ." Her voice trailed off when she opened the door and saw Bess standing there. "Oh, it's only you," she said flatly.

Bess was searching in her shoulder bag for something. "Oh, good," she said, smiling up at Leslie. "I was just looking for my room key."

"What a surprise. You're usually so organized," Leslie said dryly, eyeing the piles of books, papers, and cosmetics on Bess's desk.

Bess just giggled. Not that Leslie expected any more from her, but tonight Bess seemed even more dreamy and out of it than usual. If Wilder ever decided to hand out a prize for the biggest airhead, Leslie didn't have a doubt in the world about who would win.

"I'm really going to have to start studying more," Bess said. "It's just that until Monday's audition and the sorority rushes are over—"

"Leslie?" Tom Bowles appeared in the doorway behind Bess. His curly blond hair was messy, and he looked as if he'd been hurrying. "Great! I found you." He looked back and forth between her and Bess. "Am I interrupting something?"

"No!" Leslie said right away.

"Not at all," Bess added, going over to her bed and dropping her shoulder bag on it.

Leslie frowned when she saw the way Tom followed Bess with his eyes. "Tom Bowles, this is my roommate, Bess Marvin," she said.

She couldn't believe it when Tom actually followed Bess across the room with a disgusting puppy-dog look on his face. Bess wasn't the serious, intelligent kind of girl Leslie thought he'd be interested in.

"Oh, yeah? Hi," he said.

"Did you bring the handouts?" Leslie said loudly to get his attention.

"Right." Tom blinked, then unzipped his backpack and handed her a pile of photocopied papers. "Thanks a lot for helping me with the premed workshop. It's a huge load off my shoulders."

Leslie had been psyched when Tom had asked her to help organize a workshop for other freshmen interested in pursuing careers in medicine. It wasn't that she was surprised. After all, her high-school record was so good that she'd placed out of almost every introductory science course. Deep down, she hoped that his interest in her wasn't just academic.

"Let's see. Reading lists, resources, hospitals and research facilities where Wilder students have interned in the past." Leslie scanned the material.

"I need you to make a couple hundred copies of those, plus find a slide projector," Tom said.

"We can meet next week to take care of any last-minute details."

"Sounds good," Leslie said, and noticed that he had already turned back to Bess.

"So, Bess, what are you into?" Tom asked, propping a sneaker up on Bess's bed.

"Mmm, drama," Bess murmured. She was so busy flipping through her copy of *Grease!* that she hardly noticed him.

"Of course, Bess is barely keeping up with her classes," Leslie put in. "But you can't expect someone like her to put the same emphasis on studying that we do."

Leslie caught the wounded look on Bess's face. Maybe it was a cheap shot, but she didn't regret it. One way or another, she had to get Tom to see Bess for the airhead she really was.

Nancy stood next to Ned's beat-up green sedan in the student parking lot near Thayer Hall. The lights overhead cast a hazy yellow glow over everything.

"I can't believe this is happening," she murmured, rubbing her arms. "I keep thinking we're in some sci-fi flick where reality is totally distorted."

Ned locked the car door, then dropped the key into his jacket pocket. "This isn't a movie, Nancy," he finally said. For the briefest second, he met her gaze. Then he shoved his hands in his pockets and started toward Thayer Hall.

Now that they'd actually broken up, Nancy

hardly knew what to say to him. Catching up to Ned, she told him, "You can probably sleep in one of the lounges on the second floor—it's a guys' floor." She couldn't seem to stop babbling, saying anything to fill the awful silences.

"Okay."

Their footsteps crunched on the gravel. After a few moments, Ned said, "I'll leave early in the morning. I've got a lot of studying to do."

"Me, too," she murmured. It made sense. This was what she wanted—to be truly on her own and make a fresh start. But as Ned's long stride carried him ahead of her, Nancy felt a huge, empty space open up inside of her.

As Nancy pushed through the door to Suite 301 she noticed it wasn't even midnight, but she felt as if it were much later.

"What a day," she murmured as she opened the door to the suite.

It had been embarrassing to ask the guys on the second floor if Ned could sleep there. No one had said anything, but she could tell they thought it was pretty weird that he wasn't staying in her suite.

The lounge was dark and empty—everyone must be out partying or already asleep for the night. For once, it was actually peaceful in there. Sinking down into the mushy couch, Nancy sighed. After all that had happened, she just wanted to sit by herself for a minute.

"Nancy?"

Nancy straightened up to see Dawn Steiger, her suite's RA, standing next to the bathroom door in an oversize red T-shirt.

"What are you doing sitting in the dark?" Dawn asked. "By yourself, no less. Where's your boyfriend, Ned?"

"Sleeping on the second floor. We broke up," Nancy said flatly.

"What?" Dawn came over and sat next to her. "Are you okay?"

Am I okay? Nancy wondered. "It's weird," she admitted. "Ever since I got to Wilder I've been feeling like Ned and I weren't going to make it."

"But?" Dawn prompted.

"We went together for a long time," Nancy said slowly. "I guess I always thought it would be forever. It's scary to give that up."

"That's for sure," Dawn said, giving Nancy a sympathetic smile. "I felt exactly the same way about Peter. I was sure we were going to get married, have kids." A sad, faraway look came into her eyes. "I guess a part of me is still hoping that will happen, even though we broke up."

Nancy nodded. "Like that old song says, breaking up is hard to do."

"Hokey, but true," Dawn agreed. "I should have seen the writing on the wall. I mean, I decided that nothing could get between us. But Peter is a guy with some serious baggage from his past." She let out an abrupt laugh. "Talk about naive."

Nancy stared at Dawn. Baggage? What was she talking about?

She wouldn't have thought it was possible to feel any more confused than she did, but just hearing Peter Goodwin's name sent a slight buzz through her. She hadn't told anyone about the nerve-jangling spark that flashed between her and Peter whenever they were together. Certainly not Dawn.

I don't have any spare brain cells to think about this right now, she thought wearily. Glancing at Dawn, she said, "Maybe breaking up will turn out to be for the best."

Talk about lame. Dawn didn't seem to notice. All at once the older girl shook herself, turned to Nancy, and said, "Hey, I'm supposed to be helping you, remember?"

"Don't worry about me. I'll be fine," Nancy said. I hope, she added to herself.

"Well, okay." Dawn started toward the bathroom again, then paused in the doorway. "Just one more thing. Before you let Ned walk out of your life for good, make sure that breaking up with him is what you really want."

As Dawn disappeared inside the bathroom, Nancy felt a tiny doubt start to form in the back of her mind. It all happened so fast. She knew that breaking up was the right thing, but she didn't feel good about walking away from what she'd had without, well, without something else to take its place.

Maybe I should talk to him again, she thought.

Taking a deep breath, she got up from the couch and headed for the stairs. On the second floor, the doorway to Suite 201 was propped open. She was about to head down the hall to the lounge, when a guy's voice caught her attention. It was coming from one of the phone booths set into the wall off the second-floor landing.

"Calm down. I said I'd get you the money, and I will!" the guy said. A headful of brown hair was visible through the booth's glass door. Even though Nancy couldn't see his face, she could hear the nervousness in his voice.

"Look, you don't have to threaten me!" the guy burst out. "I *know* you fronted me the money for last week's bet. I *know* I lost the bet. I *know* I owe you."

Betting? What's up? Nancy wondered. It almost sounds as if this guy is talking to a bookie.

After a short pause the guy spoke again. Only this time, he sounded more scared than angry. "I get the picture," he said. "Either I pay up after the big game, or else!"

CHAPTER 5

Nancy stopped in her tracks. Whoa! It sounded as if the guy in the phone booth was being threatened. From what she'd heard, she guessed he was in way over his head. The stakes must be pretty high.

Her mind was spinning. Sure, college sports were big business. Everyone knew that. But gambling and physical threats at Wilder?

The door to the phone booth opened, rousing Nancy from her thoughts. The guy who came out looked incredibly tense. He shot Nancy a glance, then headed for the door leading to Suite 203.

Before she even knew what she was doing, Nancy strode over to the guy. "Hi! I couldn't help overhearing you just now," she said.

The guy's startled expression darkened to a glower. "What do you want, a medal?"

Obviously, he wasn't thrilled that a total stranger had overheard him. Not that she blamed him. A tiny voice in the back of Nancy's mind told her to let it go, to drop the whole thing and talk to Ned, as she'd planned. But something just wouldn't let her. She had to find out what was going on here.

Plastering a bright smile on her face, she said, "Hey, it's not like I'm with campus security or anything. In fact, my boyfriend and I are big Norsemen fans, but we don't know how to get any action." She lowered her voice and looked around. "You know, betting."

She could practically see the alarm bells going off inside the guy's head. "Look, this isn't some Mickey Mouse game," he told her. "I don't know what you think you heard, but—"

"I can handle the big leagues," Nancy cut in. "What's the matter? You're afraid to let someone else in on your action?"

He shot her a piercing look, trying to decide whether or not he could trust her, Nancy figured. Keep cool, she told herself. Act like you can handle it.

"It's your funeral," he muttered at last. Pulling a matchbook from his pocket, he scrawled a number on it and handed it to her. "Just tell whoever answers that Ryan said to call."

Ned had been staring glumly at the ceiling of Suite 201's lounge when he heard Nancy out on the landing. He'd been lying on the sofa, wondering if they'd just made a huge mistake, if maybe they could work things out after all. When he heard her voice, he thought that maybe she wanted to try again, too.

So what's she doing talking to some *other* guy? A quick hello on her way in would be one thing, but they'd been talking for—Ned checked the clock on the lounge wall—almost ten minutes.

He propped himself up on one elbow, but he couldn't see her or the guy. Their words were just a muffled buzz, but Nancy's tone was so hushed and secretive. What was up with her?

Don't even try to figure it out, he told himself. You and Nancy are in different places in your lives right now. He let out a sigh, flopping back against the lumpy cushion he'd been using as a pillow.

Nancy's quiet laugh floated in toward him. He knew that sound so well. He thought he knew her so well.

Stop kidding yourself, Nickerson. It's over. She's out there with another guy already. She's moved on.

He blinked at the clock again and pushed himself to sit up. So why don't I get on with it? It's not like I'm going to get any sleep tonight, even if I stick around. And the uncomfortable goodbyes tomorrow morning—does either of us really need that?

Grabbing one of his high-tops, Ned shoved his foot into it. I'll call from Emerson tomorrow to explain.

Peter Goodwin took off his jean jacket as he breezed into Thayer Hall's lobby. Maybe studying wasn't the coolest way to spend a Friday night, but at least it got him away from the freshmen frenzy. They were so overeager, falling all over themselves with that clever, sophisticated, experienced act—everything they weren't.

Peter had gotten that out of his system two years ago, when he was a freshman. He couldn't wait until the administration straightened out his rooming mix-up and moved him into one of the upperclass dorms, away from this zoo.

And away from Dawn.

Peter shook his head, letting his breath out in a rush. *Why did I let things go so far! Hadn't I already learned the hard way that getting too serious with a woman only leads to trouble?*

He'd sworn to himself never to let that happen again. Then he'd met Dawn, and she was so beautiful and sweet and smart.

"Oh—" Peter was up the stairs and practically on top of Nancy before he saw her, leaning against the wall next to the phone booths on the landing. "Sorry, I didn't see you."

"Hmm?" She barely glanced up at him. "I was, uh, thinking about making a phone call," she said distractedly, staring at a matchbook. Then she turned and started up the stairs. "Well—good night."

Peter didn't even realize he was staring at her until she disappeared into the third-floor landing. *Get a grip,* he thought. *You're not shopping, remember? Besides, she's taken.*

He was about to head into the suite when a tall, dark-haired guy with a backpack barreled toward him. "Aren't you Nancy Drew's boyfriend?" Peter asked.

The guy stopped short, did a double take. "Not anymore," he said, his eyes flashing moodily. Then he stepped around Peter and started down the stairs.

Peter stared at Ned's retreating figure, then looked up toward the third-floor landing. Hmmm . . . Sounds like a breakup. This could change everything.

As soon as the thought crossed his mind, he slammed on the mental brakes. No way. Absolutely not. Remember what happened with Dawn? Stay neutral.

With Nancy, he had a feeling that was not going to be easy.

George threw her hands in the air and cheered along with the ten thousand other fans who filled Wilder's Holliston Stadium Saturday afternoon. "Way to go, Scooter!" she yelled.

"Did you see that?" she asked, turning to Nancy and Bess. "He threw for twenty yards."

"He's amazing," Bess agreed. "And to think that tonight he's going to be your date."

George hadn't forgotten. It was kind of exciting to think about getting to know the most awesome athlete on campus. But she didn't look at him the way a lot of other girls seemed to—as if he was some kind of romantic idol.

"Listen, you guys," Nancy said, cutting into George's thoughts. "I need to finish getting the quotes I need for my article. Then I'd like to go back to my dorm to write up my notes. I'm kind of tired." Her voice sounded weary.

"What do you still need?" George asked.

"Let's see." Nancy skimmed the list she'd made. "I've spoken to one cheerleader and half a dozen students."

"Including Pam and Jamal," George said, nodding up into the stands, where her roommate was sitting with her boyfriend.

Nancy nodded. "So now I need to find someone who looks like an alum, and I want to get a quote from the mascot."

"George and I could do it," Bess offered. "I mean, you've been through a lot. Breaking up with Ned and everything."

"That's exactly why I'm glad I have to do this," Nancy said. "It keeps my mind off the fact that I just broke up with a guy I've been in love with practically forever."

She was trying to be cheerful, but George noticed the circles under her eyes. Nancy couldn't have slept much the night before, and George couldn't begin to imagine what Nancy was going through. Even if things *had* been shaky for her with Ned, breaking up couldn't be easy. "Well, if you want to talk..." George offered.

"Thanks, but I don't really know what's left to say," Nancy told her. "It's weird. I want to think about Ned and what's happened, but my mind keeps jumping to everything and anything else." She sighed, then added, "I guess that's a sign that our breaking up wasn't such a bad idea."

The three girls were silent for a minute. Finally Bess asked, "So, Nan, are you going to call the phone number that guy gave you for betting?"

George shook her head. "I guess I shouldn't be so surprised that there's gambling going on here," she said. "With a team as hot as the Norsemen, it's inevitable."

"And illegal," Nancy reminded her. "I haven't called yet, but—"

A collective gasp rose from the crowd. George turned to check the action on the field. "Oh, no! They're trying to sack him." She bit her lip as the Chargers' tackles closed in on Scooter. At the last second he twisted around them, pulled free, and threw to a receiver near the end zone. The pass was completed, and the ball was at the fifteen-yard line.

The entire stadium went crazy. George couldn't help feeling a thrill. If only she could get rid of her guilty thoughts about canceling her date with Will.

The stadium uproar was just dying down when Nancy saw the Viking mascot take off his horned helmet and walk away from the sidelines.

"Oh! The Viking is taking a break," she told

Bess and George. "Let me see if I can get a quote from him."

The truth was, even though she was glad for her friends' support, she felt funny talking about Ned. Everything had happened so fast—the breakup, and then his leaving without saying goodbye. Until she had time to get used to it, she didn't really want to discuss it—even with George and Bess.

It took only a few minutes to get a quote from the mascot. Nancy was about to rejoin Bess and George at the edge of the bleachers, when she spotted Gail Gardeski in the refreshment line.

"Hi," Nancy said, stepping over to Gail. "Do you have a second? I want to ask you something."

Gail's gaze flickered over Nancy's notepad and mini-recorder. "Sure," she said. "Let me get something to drink first, okay?"

Nancy waited at the edge of the refreshment area. The stadium was charged with extra-high-voltage energy. Victory was in the air. She could see it on the faces of everyone heading to and from the concessions stands.

Jamal's striking face materialized above the crowd. He was talking to a heavyset guy wearing a Brockton Cougars jacket. Conspiring with the enemy, eh? Nancy thought, smiling. Some of the Cougars must be here taking notes for their game next week against Wilder. She was about to call out to him, when someone tapped her on the shoulder.

"Nancy?"

Gail Gardeski was standing right next to her, holding a big plastic cup with a picture of a Viking on it. "Did something go wrong during your interview with Scooter?" she asked worriedly.

"The interview went fine," Nancy assured her. "I'll have it for you first thing tomorrow, along with my other assignment."

Gail frowned at her. "That's not good enough. I told you I needed that interview today."

"I know. I had some, uh, personal problems," Nancy said. "I couldn't get to it."

Uh-oh. So far this conversation wasn't going the way she'd hoped. Before Gail could say anything else, Nancy quickly added, "Actually, what I wanted to talk to you about was an investigative article I thought might be good for the paper." She glanced around to make sure no one could overhear her. "About big-time gambling on campus."

Lowering her voice, Nancy quickly filled Gail in on the phone call she'd overheard the night before. "I have a hunch that—"

"A hunch?" Gail interrupted. "You can't write an article based on hunches, Nancy. Serious reporters need hard facts."

"I know," Nancy said quickly. "But I'm sure that with a little more digging—"

"Just what I need," Gail said, rolling her eyes. "Why don't you meet the deadlines you have before you try to become the next Lois Lane. I expect to see your interview *and* the quotes from today's game on my desk in the newspaper office first thing tomorrow morning."

With that, Gail walked back toward the bleachers and disappeared into the crowd.

Nancy just stood there, staring at the spot where Gail had been. In her entire life, no one had ever treated her like such a—novice.

Behind her, another roar rose from the bleachers. Cries of "Touchdown!" echoed in the air as the band started to play. But Nancy hardly heard.

"Facts, huh?" she murmured, clenching her notepad and recorder more tightly. "If that's what you want, then that's what I'll get."

This was it, the moment he'd been waiting for—Wilder's first touchdown. He watched as Berenson, unable to unload the ball, made a seemingly effortless fifteen-yard run down the line to score. The crowd was going wild.

Now he gripped the binoculars, focused on the quarterback's face. "Go ahead, Scooter. Spike it," he urged under his breath. "Spike it!"

Scooter was pumped, he could tell that much. The quarterback raised the ball above his head. Yes! He's going to do it!

Then, suddenly, a change came over Scooter. His entire body tightened. Instead of spiking the ball, he drop-kicked it away from the goal. His defiant stance made Scooter's message all the more clear.

The young man lowered the binoculars, his rage seething. So, Scooter had made his choice. He'd decided not to go along with the plan. Obviously, he didn't know whom he was dealing with.

But he was going to find out. The hard way.

CHAPTER 6

Bess felt the cool night air on her cheeks as she and Brian headed down the path toward Thayer Hall. "I know Nancy said she had to write up that stuff for the paper," she said. "But everyone needs a study break."

"So we're going to drag her to a frat house so she can watch a bunch of guys named Bubba smash beer cans on their heads." Brian's green eyes were sparkling with amusement. "That's not a study break—that's total insanity."

"Whatever," Bess said, laughing. "I still think it's better than letting her mope around her room all night thinking about Ned."

Brian just shrugged and kept walking. He was wearing jeans and a bomber jacket, Bess noticed. Nothing special, but since the night before, she realized she was looking at him differently.

"We're still on for tomorrow night at Hewlitt, right?" Brian asked a moment later.

"I thought we went over this before," she told him. "Do you want to get out of meeting there?"

"No. I'll be there." He said it lightly, but the laughter was gone from his eyes. In fact, he seemed almost nervous.

"Is something wrong?" Bess asked.

He shook his head. "Actually, everything is starting to be amazingly right," he said, giving her a mysterious smile.

"Meaning?" she prompted, but he just gave her that secret grin again.

Bess decided to drop it. Anyway, she was pretty sure she knew what he wanted to say. Soon enough the time would be right, and he'd be telling her that she was the only girl for him.

"Scooter! George!" Kara Verbeck materialized out of the crowd that was packed into the Beta house. She grinned and waved an instant camera in their faces. "Smile and say 'Champs!'"

George smiled halfheartedly as she felt Scooter's hand slip around her waist. "Champs," Scooter said. A second later came the blinding flash.

By the time George stopped seeing stars, Scooter was already a few feet away in a crowd of fans. He'd been so busy soaking up everyone's praise that he'd barely said two words to her since he'd picked her up at her dorm.

I guess I should have expected this, she thought, pushing down her irritation. He did pull off an awesome victory for the Norsemen. Still, she felt more like an ornament than Scooter's date. He put an arm around her whenever one of his frat brothers was around. But so far he hadn't shown much interest in actually talking to her.

Not that conversation was easy in this madhouse. Bodies were jammed together in the large open room off the foyer. Music blared from two huge speakers. A steady stream of people flowed through the halls to the kitchen, where the beer, soda, and munchies were. Even the stairway, where George and Scooter were now standing, was crammed with people going to and from the bathrooms upstairs.

George looked over the wooden railing, searching for Bess and Brian. They weren't here yet, but George did see a few other people she knew. Eileen was there, dancing with a guy George didn't recognize. And she spotted a few people from Jamison.

She turned as a guy with blond hair stopped next to Scooter. "Hey, Scooter. Here's an instant replay," the guy called out. He took his empty beer can and slammed it against his forehead, completely flattening it. "That's what you guys did to the Chargers today. You were awesome!"

Scooter laughed and fingered the rabbit's foot that hung around his neck on a chain. "What can I say? The Berenson magic was working."

George decided to try to talk to him again. Smiling at Scooter, she said, "You really *were* awesome. How do you manage all those amazing moves?" She tapped his rabbit's foot. "It can't all be luck, right?"

"Who knows? Maybe it is." Scooter shrugged, his blue eyes flitting around Beta house.

Was this guy for real? "You're probably right. Training, strategy, natural talent. That stuff probably doesn't have anything to do with your success," she said.

"Actually, I'm thinking of dropping the training part," Scooter said, grinning at her. "I'm sure the coach'll understand."

"Not!" they both said at once.

At least he had a sense of humor. "Coaches aren't exactly the sentimental types," George said. "I remember one time when my high-school track team was training for—"

"Can't we forget about sports for a while?" Scooter cut in, frowning. "I get enough shop talk around here. Besides—" he reached around George's waist and gave her a little squeeze— "most girls are more interested in what I'm like off the field."

George twisted away from him, feeling her cheeks start to burn. "Look, I need to get something to drink," she told him.

"What?" he shouted over the music, but George could see that he wasn't really listening. He was grinning and looking everywhere at once. Of course it would only take about two seconds before some girl would go up to him and start babbling about how great he'd played that day.

"I'll be back in a minute!" George called.

It was a relief to be away from him. As she threaded her way past the raucous crowd on the stairs, she let out a sigh. Scooter obviously didn't think a girl was capable of talking intelligently about sports. For such a talented guy, he was seriously dense when it came to understanding women.

"Aren't you here with Scooter Berenson?" a girl's voice broke into George's thoughts. The girl was petite with long dark hair, and the expression on her face was openly envious.

"Yeah," George answered. "Do you know him?"

"I wish," the girl said, reaching for a can of beer. "You don't know how lucky you are."

Stupid is more like it, thought George. "Trust me," she said dryly, "lucky doesn't begin to describe how I feel right now."

"I can't believe I let you talk me into coming here!" Nancy shouted as she, Bess, and Brian stepped into the Beta house.

"It is kind of crazy," Bess admitted. "But it's supposed to be. This is a victory party, after all!"

"At least I don't see anyone wearing a toga," Brian said.

Nancy couldn't help laughing. "Actually, I think *I* take the prize for weird looks." She waved at Kara's red suede jacket, which was way too short on her. Her violet shirt stuck out awkwardly from the bottom of it. Peeling off the jacket, Nancy tossed it in a corner of the foyer.

"If anyone sees Kara, be sure to get my leather jacket from her."

"Sure," Bess said. Her eyes flitted eagerly over the crowd inside. "Oh—I think I see George. I'm going to get the scoop on what's up with her and Scooter. Back in a minute."

As Bess disappeared into the pack, Nancy and Brian stepped into the living room. Stephanie was standing near the stairs, Nancy saw, looking as sultry as ever. She was dressed in black shorts, a skintight striped shirt, and thigh-high stockings, which left a strip of skin showing beneath her shorts.

"As if you don't know that every guy in sight is drooling at you," Nancy murmured about Stephanie.

"What?" Brian asked.

"Oh—nothing," Nancy said. "I'll be right back, Brian. There's something I have to do."

So much had been happening, she'd almost forgotten about Stephanie's flirting with Ned the night before. Almost, but not quite.

Stephanie raised one of her dark eyebrows when she saw Nancy. "Well, if it isn't Thayer Hall's very own fairy-tale princess."

Nancy ignored the sarcasm in Stephanie's voice. "Why did you tell lies about me to Ned?" she demanded. "Didn't you think I'd find out about them?"

"Lies?" Stephanie's eyes widened in an innocent look that made Nancy want to punch her.

"Surely you know what the word means,"

Nancy said, keeping her voice even. "Or maybe you thought you were doing me some kind of favor when you told Ned that I've been seeing other guys, that I was acting like he wasn't even my boyfriend."

Stephanie didn't bat an eye. "From what I can tell, he's not your boyfriend anymore, is he?"

She's smooth, I'll give her that, Nancy thought. But Stephanie's smug attitude only made her angrier. "That's not the point. You deliberately tried to sabotage my relationship with Ned and—"

"You're blowing this way out of proportion," Stephanie cut in. "Really, Nancy, whatever's going on between you and Prince Charming is none of my business." She let her eyes wander lazily over the crowd. "Besides, don't you have to get back to the dorm before you turn into a pumpkin or something?"

Nancy opened her mouth to speak, but she didn't get the chance.

"There's Peter," Stephanie went on, nodding toward the door. "I think I'll go say hi."

A second later she was gone. Nancy let her breath out in a frustrated rush. Why did she let Stephanie get to her like that?

Turning around, she saw Peter standing in the foyer, taking off his jacket. He looked over the crowd, and his eyes locked on hers for a brief moment. Then Stephanie was beside him, blocking her view.

Don't let it bother you, Nancy ordered herself.

But seeing the intimate way Stephanie slid up to Peter, she couldn't help feeling a pang of jealousy.

"Peter!" Stephanie exclaimed, giving him a kiss on the cheek. "Finally, someone whose brain cells aren't smashed into the football field. I'm so happy to have someone halfway intelligent to talk to."

Glancing over her shoulder, she saw Nancy's face fall, just the slightest bit. Perfect.

Peter blinked at her. "Don't you live in my dorm?" he asked, taking her in.

"Stephanie Keats," she reminded him. "I'm in Suite 301. We've met a few times, remember?"

"Mmm," Peter murmured absentmindedly. Then his eyes flitted toward the stairs and he asked, "Weren't you just talking to Nancy Drew?"

Wrong answer, Stephanie thought. "Who?" she asked. "Oh, never mind, I'm sure we can—"

"Hey, you two!" Kara called out. "You're on *Candid Camera!*"

Seeing the camera Kara held, Stephanie hooked her arm through Peter's and pressed her cheek against his. "Smile, now," she said.

I know I am. Eat your heart out, Nancy Drew.

"Thanks," Kara told Stephanie and Peter after snapping the picture. Turning away from them, she tucked the camera under her arm and scanned the dance floor. Where was Vic?

Finally she spotted him. He was standing in the hall near the kitchen, holding a plastic cup filled with beer. She couldn't help smiling when she saw his big brown eyes and the unruly curl of dark hair that always fell across his forehead. Kara hurried over to him, before he could disappear again. "Hi," she said, planting a kiss on his cheek. "Where've you been?"

"Around. I had to make a phone call," Vic told her. He gave a shrug as if it wasn't a big deal. But he seemed nervous, on edge.

"Hey, relax," she said. What was with him tonight? she wondered. He kept looking around, as if he were waiting for someone. "You guys won today, remember? And you played flawlessly," she said.

At least that got a smile out of him. "Thanks for reminding me," he said, taking her hand and twining his fingers with hers. "Of course, I did only play the last five minutes of the game."

Kara knew that it wasn't easy being in Scooter Berenson's shadow. But that didn't make Vic any less of a hero to her. "You were great," she said, throwing her arms around him. Then she stepped back and aimed her camera at him. "How about a snapshot for your biggest fan? Smile!"

But when she looked through the viewfinder at him, he was glowering at her. "Lighten up," she told him. "That face looks like it belongs on a mug shot."

She thought he'd at least chuckle, but instead his whole body went taut. "What did you say?"

He practically growled the question. Lowering her camera again, Kara walked slowly back to him. She could feel tears filling her eyes. "What's gotten into you, Vic?" she whispered.

The expression in his eyes immediately softened. "Hey, I'm sorry. I'm just tense now. We're under a lot of pressure to be champs, and—"

"It's okay," she told him. "I don't like to see you unhappy, that's all."

Vic stroked her cheek with his thumb. "Sorry," he said again. "I shouldn't take it out on you. You're the best thing that's happened to me."

Leaning forward, he gave Kara a kiss that sent a delicious shiver through her. Everything's fine, she told herself firmly. Everything's better than fine.

"See you, Bess. Thanks for listening."

George waved as Bess left the crowded kitchen and headed back to the dance floor. Scooter was still standing on the stairs, surrounded by people. She'd been avoiding him for over a half hour while she complained to Bess about what a waste her date was. She realized she couldn't hide behind the tortilla chips forever.

Taking a deep breath, she began threading her way back toward Scooter. She was almost to the stairs, when the front door opened and a couple came in. The blast of cool, moist air that gusted in with them was inviting. Irresistible.

I'll just head out for a minute, she thought.

Scooter won't mind. He's so wrapped up in himself, he probably won't even notice.

George quickly stepped around the couple and went outside. It was drizzling, but she didn't care. Standing on the porch, she leaned on the railing and took a deep breath.

What a total failure of a Saturday night. Well, I guess this is what I get for canceling on Will. Reap what you sow, and all that.

"George?" Scooter's voice sounded behind her. She turned to see the quarterback standing on the porch. "Where are you going?" he asked.

"I needed some fresh air," she told him. "Actually, I think I might call it a night."

"You're going? So soon?" Scooter asked, frowning. He came over and put his arm around her. "But we were just getting to know each other."

George had to roll her eyes at that one. "Yeah, well, um, I'm really tired and—"

Out of the corner of her eye, she noticed two guys walking along the street near Beta. Suddenly she felt a prickly feeling at the back of her neck. George's breath caught in her throat as she turned her head and recognized Will Blackfeather's tall silhouette.

Please don't let him see me, she begged.

It was too late. Will had stopped. And he was staring right at her.

CHAPTER 7

I don't believe this," Will said under his breath. There was George with Scott Berenson wrapped around her like a second skin.

"What's up, buddy?" Andy stopped a few steps ahead of Will and looked back at him. "You look as if you've seen a ..." His voice trailed off as he followed Will's gaze. "Uh-oh. Is that who I think it is?"

George was peering over Scooter's shoulder, and her whole face froze when she saw Will.

"I don't need this." Will shoved his hands in his pockets and stormed down the street with a vengeance. "Something came up, huh?" he muttered.

"Hey, buddy!" Andy called, jogging to catch up with him. "Are you all right?"

Will barely heard his roommate. "I actually thought she liked me," he went on, keeping his eyes down. "It's pretty obvious what she was really up to."

"Up to?" Andy's perplexed, slightly out of breath voice came from beside him. "Hey, Will, slow down. We're not training for a marathon, you know."

"She was just stringing me along this whole time, keeping me on standby," Will said bitterly, shaking his head. "I was being dangled in case things didn't work out with Berenson. And here I was actually trying to help her with this whole Selective Service thing."

"Will! Wait a second!"

Will stopped, blinking at the exasperation in Andy's voice. "What?" he asked.

"Aren't you jumping to conclusions?" Andy asked. "I mean, maybe her dinner ended early. Maybe she stopped by for some chips and conversation."

"I didn't see much talking going on," Will shot back.

"Ouch," Andy said, grimacing. "Look, all I'm trying to say is that you haven't even heard her side of things yet."

Will wasn't sure he wanted to. He'd heard enough lies from Angela. He could do without more lame excuses. "I know everything I need to," he muttered. "From now on, I'm steering clear of her."

"Bess!" Nancy squeezed around a dancing couple and tapped Bess on the shoulder. Bess and Brian stopped dancing, their faces red and glowing.

"I'm going back to the dorm," Nancy shouted.

Bess looked as if she was going to protest, but Brian stopped her. "Bye, Nancy!" he yelled. "Say good night, Bess," he said firmly.

Bess laughed and waved at Nancy. "Good night, Bess!" she called. Then she started dancing again.

"What a couple of nut cases," Nancy murmured as she headed for the foyer. Kara's red suede jacket was easy to find in the pile of lightweight sweaters and blazers. Nancy thrust an arm into one sleeve, twisting toward the door at the same time.

"Oh—sorry!" she said as she felt her hand hit someone. She glanced at the other person, then did a double take. "Peter! You're leaving?"

He pretended to think about the question. "Let's see. I'm getting my jacket, heading for the door. Yes!" he said, shooting her a teasing grin. "I am leaving."

"You're sure, now?" she asked.

Peter nodded, pointing at some wet spots on his shirt and jeans. "I go by the quota system. No more than three beers spilled on me at any one party. Especially when I'm not drinking. What's your excuse?" he asked, holding the door for her.

As she brushed past him, Nancy felt oddly self-conscious, as if she were somehow betraying Ned. "I didn't think I needed one," she said lightly, trying to cover her nervousness. "But if you must know, I have two pieces due on Gail Gardeski's desk by tomorrow morning, or my career as a reporter for the *Wilder Times* will be the shortest in Wilder's history."

"Ah—something else I didn't know about you," Peter commented as they headed toward the dorm. "A reporter, eh?"

"Just one of my many talents," she said, buffing her nails on Kara's jacket sleeve. She tried not to notice his strong, handsome features, the way his dark eyes played over her face. "But I'm sure you must have a few of your own," she added. "Talents, I mean."

"Oh, no, you don't. I'm not falling for that trick." Peter shot her a sidelong glance. "I know how you reporters operate. Tonight you get me to pour my heart out and tomorrow it's all over the front pa—"

All at once he stopped talking, his eyes frozen on something to their right. Following his gaze, Nancy saw Dawn Steiger about twenty yards away. When she saw Peter and Nancy, Dawn's whole body tensed. She stopped for just an instant. Then she jogged away, taking the path that led toward Thayer Hall.

Good going, Nancy thought. Dawn just finished telling you how hard it is for her to be around Peter. Now, practically two seconds later, she sees me joking around with her ex.

Joking? a tiny voice prompted. Or flirting? Watch your step, or things could get pretty tense in Suite 301.

* * *

Peter watched Dawn disappear down the path. Why did he suddenly feel so guilty, so confused and self-conscious? Breaking up had been hard but inevitable. Things were getting too serious, he just couldn't handle it. Even Dawn had agreed that breaking up was best, especially once she'd found out the truth about him.

Not that she was happy about it. Far from it. But at least she understood, or at least he thought she did.

He gazed at Nancy. They'd just been talking, no big deal. But he knew how quickly things could get out of control.

He'd get to know her better, then things would heat up. And before he could put on the brakes, she'd find out what he swore no one at Wilder would ever know.

"Peter, are you all right?" Nancy asked.

Fat chance. Peter stared at the ground, the trees, anywhere but into her deep blue eyes. "I, uh, just remembered that I have to be someplace," he said.

Good one, he thought. Very smooth.

He didn't bother waiting for her reaction. Turning, he strode the other way down the street.

George Fayne, you are a total idiot!

Scooter had talked her into coming back inside Beta. She was going through the motions of dancing, but it wasn't easy. Not when she kept picturing Will's face when he'd seen her and Scooter. And then he'd taken off before she could explain.

80

Of course she had no explanation that made sense. The truth was, she deserved his contempt.

Right next to her Scooter was jumping and twisting to the beat. He didn't even seem to notice that she was upset.

George stopped dancing and tapped Scooter on the shoulder. "Scooter! I'm going back to my dorm. I'm not feeling so great," she told him. It wasn't a lie. Every time she thought about Will, she felt sick to her stomach.

"The party's just getting going," he objected. "You can't go now."

"Sorry. Listen, you don't have to leave or anything," she said. "I know the way."

Scooter acted as if he was going to keep trying to talk her out of it. But then he touched her elbow and said, "I'll give you a ride."

"That's okay," George said, shaking her head.

"It's no big deal," he insisted. "I want to."

George didn't feel like standing around arguing, so she shrugged and said, "Okay. Whatever."

His white Camaro was parked right in front of Beta House. "No one can say Scott Berenson doesn't travel in style," he boasted as he opened the passenger door for her.

George gave a weary smile. "Enough about me," she mumbled. "Let's talk about *you* for a change."

"Huh?"

"Nothing." She climbed inside and settled against the plush leather seat. Just a few more minutes, she thought. Then the worst night of your life will be over.

It wasn't until after they were inside the closed car that she realized how strongly Scooter smelled of alcohol. She'd seen him holding a plastic cup at the party but hadn't thought much about what was in it.

Until now. "How many beers did you have?" she asked.

"Just enough to stay loose," Scooter answered. He grinned at her, then turned the key and gunned the engine.

Uh-oh. His speech was slurred, too. "Uh, Scooter?" George asked, leaning forward, "do you really think you should drive when—"

He shot away from the curb with the tires peeling rubber, sending George flying backward against the seat. "Hey!" she cried, grabbing frantically for her seat belt. "Stop driving like a maniac!"

Scooter just kept grinning, shifting the car into second, then third. George braced herself against the dashboard as he careened around a group of guys and girls. "I mean it, Scooter!" she cried. "You shouldn't be driving when you're—"

"Where's your sense of adventure?" he said, interrupting her.

The Camaro skidded onto a deserted side road. George squeezed her eyes shut as the rear end fishtailed dangerously close to the trees lining the road.

"I must have left it back at Beta—along with

my sanity!" she said. Even with her seat belt on, she'd bounced off the door so many times, she was starting to feel like a punching bag.

"You forgot to tell me that you have a death wish," she said through clenched teeth. "Come on—stop!"

Scooter's grin faded. "Lighten up, George. You really know how to ruin a good—"

"STOP!" she yelled.

He clamped his mouth into a tight line. "Fine. If that's what you want."

"Wait!" she cried. "Not on the curve!"

It was too late. Scooter hit the brakes, and the Camaro spun out of control, sliding down and around the bend in the road. George threw her arms out to keep from slamming into the windshield. She closed her eyes, waiting for the crash.

Finally the car jerked to a halt and she opened her eyes. The boathouse and lake were in front of her. The Camaro was stopped at an angle in the middle of the parking lot. The Camaro must have skidded all the way down to the end of the road, she thought. But, hey, at least we're still alive.

"Get out," Scooter told her.

George blinked at him. "What?"

"You heard me," he said angrily. "If you think I'm too drunk to drive, you can get out and walk!"

"From here?" she asked. "It'll take me half an hour. And it's totally deserted."

"Not my problem." Scooter reached in front

of her, unlocked the door, and flicked it open. "Most girls would jump at the chance to get me alone out here. You blew it."

George fumbled with her seat belt, feeling angrier every second. "You're really a piece of work, you know?" she told him. She got out of the Camaro, then paused to look at him. "Just for the record, if you were the only guy on campus, I wouldn't be caught dead dating you!"

Before he could answer, she slammed the car door and strode away. She was vaguely aware of another car pulling into the lot, but all her thoughts were on getting away from Scooter.

Forget about him, she thought. Forget this entire night ever happened.

Nancy reached out groggily to silence the noisy ringing of her alarm clock. She groaned when she saw how early it was. Eight-thirty. What kind of self-respecting college student gets up that early on a Sunday morning?

"You do," she murmured. "Unless you want to give Gail a reason to kick you off the paper."

She'd been up until after three finishing the articles. They weren't half bad. At least, that was what she'd thought before going to sleep. But this morning everything seemed bleaker—the gray sky outside, her boring desk and dresser, Kara's empty bed.

Apparently, Kara had spent the night at Beta. Somehow, it only made Nancy feel sadder about her own life. Shaking herself, she got out of bed, put on her bathrobe, and grabbed her shampoo and towel.

Nancy groaned when she pushed open the bathroom door and saw Stephanie standing there in tights and a T-shirt. An army of cleansers, creams, and cosmetics were lined up on the shelf in front of her. She looked at Nancy but didn't say anything. Fine with me, thought Nancy. She headed for the showers.

By the time she walked into the lounge a half hour later, she was feeling halfway human again. "Hi, Ginny. Hi, Liz," she called, when she saw the two girls come out of their room.

"Morning," Ginny said. "Feel like some eggs and toast?"

"Sounds tempting," Nancy said, grimacing. "I'll skip the eggs, but I could use some caffeine. Wait for me while I get dressed, okay?"

"Did someone say caffeine?" Reva stuck her head out of the room she shared with Eileen. She yawned, then stepped into the hall, wearing a robe.

Liz nodded. "Want us to wait for you and Eileen?"

"Nah. I'll stop at Java Joe's for a quick fix on my way to the library," Reva said. "I wouldn't bother waiting for that girl." She nodded at the motionless lump under the blankets in Eileen's bed. "She didn't get back from Beta until after four."

"Now, there's a woman who knows how to

party," Ginny said, grinning. "We should be taking lessons."

Nancy started to laugh, but the sound stuck in her throat when she saw Dawn come out of her room.

"Hi, everyone," Dawn said, giving a half-hearted smile. Her eyes lingered on Nancy for a moment, and then she disappeared into the bathroom.

Uh-oh, thought Nancy. I hope that what happened isn't going to ruin the atmosphere around here.

She turned as the door to their suite banged open, and Kara ran in. "Did you guys hear the news?"

Suddenly everyone in the suite was talking at once. "What?" "What happened?" "Don't keep us in suspense."

Kara's face was flushed with excitement. "It's Scooter. He broke his hand—got it slammed in his car door when he was with *your* friend," she said, jabbing a finger at Nancy.

Nancy blinked, trying to figure out what Kara was talking about. "You mean George?"

Kara nodded. "Of course I mean George. Scooter's going to be out of commission for the rest of the season, and it's all her fault!"

CHAPTER 8

"Am I really about to go for another run?" George groaned as she and Pam stepped out of Jamison Hall and into the bright morning sunshine. "I put in my jogging time running back here from the boathouse last night."

Pam gave her a sympathetic smile. "The perfect ending to a wonderful evening?"

"Oh, yeah. Absolutely," George answered. She stopped in the grass next to the dorm and began doing warm-up exercises. "Not only did I have the honor of dating the most arrogant, reckless jerk on campus. I've also totally wrecked things with a guy I really care about." She rolled her eyes, first stretching her left leg, then her right. "I'm so happy I could just burst into song."

"Please, not that," Pam said in mock horror. "*I'm* not the one who dumped you halfway across campus."

George had already given Pam a blow-by-blow

description of her entire disastrous date. Her stomach still twisted into knots every time she thought about Will. But talking about it had at least helped her to see how ridiculous the situation with Scooter had been.

"My voice isn't that bad," George objected. Shooting Pam a challenging grin, she darted down the path toward the main quad.

"Hey!" Pam called. She caught up with George. "I thought we were training for a race, not actually running one," she said breathlessly.

"You know what they say, no pain, no gain," George quipped, but she slowed her pace. "Sorry. I guess I feel like I have to punish myself for what happened," she admitted.

Pam just rolled her eyes. "Scooter's the one who should be punished, not—"

"That's not what I'm talking about," George cut in. "I mean for the way I treated Will. He must hate me."

"Not necessarily," Pam put in. "Maybe he's not as mad as you think. If you could just—"

She stopped talking and frowned at a group of girls they'd just passed on the quad. "Why are they looking at us like that?" she murmured.

"Like what?" George turned, jogging in place, so she could see them better. Three girls were hunched together whispering. They all glared at George before continuing down the walk the other way.

"What's their problem?" she said, frowning. "I

may have seen them around the boathouse, but it's not like I know them or anything."

Pam shrugged. "Forget about it. Let's run."

But when they jogged past Java Joe's a few minutes later, it happened again. George had the feeling that a group at one of the outdoor tables was staring at her. What was going on?

"That's the girl who did it," George heard one of them say. "She broke his hand."

George stopped in her tracks and stared at the girl. Petite . . . dark hair . . . It took George a minute to realize that it was the same girl who'd spoken to her in the kitchen at the party.

"What did you say?" George asked. When the girl wouldn't meet her gaze, George strode over to her. "Really, I'd like to know. Whose hand did I break?"

When the girl finally looked at George, her eyes were flashing defiantly. "You want me to spell it out for you?" the girl asked angrily. "Fine. First, you throw yourself at Scooter. He's not interested, but you don't take no for an answer—"

"Hold on a sec," George cut in, raising a hand. "You think that I threw myself at him?"

The girl just rolled her eyes. "As if you didn't already know," she muttered. "So how do you get back at him? You steal his lucky rabbit's foot and then slam the car door on his hand." She smirked at George. "Congratulations. You managed to break his hand."

"That's outrageous!" Pam burst out, but George barely heard her.

She blinked, as if that would somehow cancel what was happening. But when she opened her eyes the girl was still there, glaring at her.

Her head was buzzing. Who would spread such a vicious lie about her?

As soon as the question popped into her head, she knew the answer. It could only be one person.

Scooter.

Kara took in her suitemates' shocked expressions. "I couldn't believe it, either," she told them. "But I saw Scooter myself when he got back to the frat house from the emergency room this morning. He was there most of the night having his hand set."

"George would never do that," Nancy said, frowning at Kara. "Where did it happen?"

"In his car, obviously," Kara answered. "Scooter said that George started coming on to him when he drove her to her dorm. And when he said he wasn't interested . . ."

"That's crazy! George didn't even like him," Nancy burst out. "Did anyone *see* her slam the door on him? I mean, were any of you there?"

"I got to the party pretty late. I never really even saw Scooter," Ginny said, shrugging.

"Don't look at me." Reva held up her hands. "I wasn't even at the party."

"So how does anyone know that George is responsible?" Nancy pressed.

Kara stepped back from Nancy. "All these questions are giving me a serious headache," she said. "Relax, okay?"

"I just know that George would never break anyone's hand, that's all," Nancy said. "Are you sure you didn't see anyone else at the party who was mad at Scooter? Or jealous?"

Kara sighed. Nancy was an okay roommate, but sometimes Kara wished she would loosen up a little. "Nancy, you've got to let go of all this"— she waved her hands in the air, searching for the right word—"negativity. It's not going to help Scooter or George."

"Spreading rumors that aren't true isn't going to help anyone, either," Nancy shot back.

"Besides, Kara, it doesn't sound as if there's a lot to be positive about," Liz Bader said wryly.

Why did people always have to focus on the down side of things? "Well, for one thing, this could mean good things for Vic," Kara said, thinking out loud. "He's a great quarterback, and now he'll get to start in the game against Brockton. It's a major opportunity for him."

She didn't want to seem insensitive about Scooter's hand, but it was pretty exciting.

"That's right," Nancy murmured. "He stands to gain a lot from Scooter's accident."

Kara was taken aback by the suspicious tone in Nancy's voice, and she suddenly felt defensive. "Hey! You don't think that . . ."

"Sounds like a motive to me," Reva said, arching an eyebrow.

"But Vic didn't do it—George did!" Kara shot back. "Why would Scooter lie?"

Some of their suitemates nodded their agreement, but Kara could tell that Nancy wasn't convinced.

Well, that's her problem, thought Kara. Not mine.

Nancy's hair was flying as she raced down Jamison Hall's fourth-floor hallway to Room 425. "George," she called, knocking on the door. "Are you there? It's me, Nancy."

The door flew open, and Bess was standing there. Behind her, George and Pam were sitting on George's bed. "You heard what happened?" Bess asked, pulling Nancy into the room.

When Nancy nodded, George dropped her head into her hands. "What did Scooter do, make an announcement on the campus radio station or something?" she groaned.

"I'm pretty sure the news flash is limited to the jocks at Beta and their friends," Nancy said. "Kara was at the house when Scooter got back. I heard the story from her. I figured I'd better come over here and find out what *really* happened."

"You mean, you don't think that George has suddenly turned into a psycho who gets her thrills by maiming campus sports stars?" Pam asked.

"That's the real me, all right," George said, grimacing. "As my oldest friends, I guess you have a right to know." She said it jokingly, but Nancy didn't miss the troubled look in her brown eyes.

"So what did happen?" Nancy asked. "How did such a crazy rumor get started?"

She sat down at George's desk, listening while the others filled her in. When they were done, she just shook her head.

"This still doesn't make sense to me," she said. "I mean, all that happened was that you asked Scooter not to drive when he'd been drinking, right?"

George nodded. "But he went ballistic and practically killed us while stopping the car, and then he kicked me out."

"Sensitive guy," Pam commented. "Do you know where I can meet someone like him?"

"You already have a boyfriend, remember?" George put in. "Seriously, I've been thinking a lot about this. Maybe I did slam the car door, but I'm pretty sure I didn't break his hand."

"You didn't hear him yell or anything?" Bess asked.

"Nope." George gave a firm shake of her head. "I wasn't paying close attention, but I still think I would have sensed *something* if I'd slammed his hand in the door."

Nancy drummed her fingers on George's desk, thinking. "So, you probably didn't break Scooter's hand," she said. "But someone did. And for some reason Scooter lied about it and said it was you."

"Maybe it was an accident," Bess suggested. "That was a crazy party. Scooter could have done something stupid and then blamed George so that he wouldn't have to admit to being a klutz and letting everyone down right before the big game."

It was possible, but . . . "There's no way we'll figure out what really happened unless we have more to go on," Nancy said. She looked around the room. "Anyone up for heading over to the boathouse?"

The young man stood by the boathouse, staring at the parking lot. He'd anticipated that there might be problems with the girl. That was why he'd come back here, to make sure nothing had been left behind that would incriminate him. He'd clean up those tracks . . .

Suddenly he heard voices coming from the top of the drive. He ducked inside the boathouse. He didn't need anyone finding him and suspecting he had something to do with Scooter's "accident." He smiled to himself, fingering Scooter's rabbit's foot. Still, if someone did get too close, there were ways to get them out of the way—permanently. He crouched noiselessly inside the boathouse, listening.

"So this is the scene of the crime?" Nancy said twenty minutes later. She, Bess, and George were looking down the final curve in the drive that led to the boathouse. As the road dipped toward the parking lot, the gravel thinned to a sea of dried, pockmarked mud.

"Looks more like one of those places where they hold demolition derbies," Bess put in. Shading her eyes from the sun, she pointed to a set of long, sliding tire tracks that fishtailed down the hill to the parking lot. "Check out those skid marks."

"Scooter," George said, frowning. "That's where he decided to impress me with his amazing ability to trash his car and practically kill us both."

"What a talented guy," Bess said as they picked their way down the hill to the spot where the skid marks ended. "And you didn't fall for it? What kind of devoted groupie are you?"

"One who wanted to get out of here—fast," George said. She pointed to some footprints leading away from the parking lot where the car had stopped. "Those are mine," she said. "I still haven't gotten the mud off my shoes."

"At least last night's damp weather was good for something," Nancy said, looking around. "The tracks are really clear." She pointed to a second set of tire marks. They ended about ten feet from where Scooter had stopped. "Looks like Scooter wasn't the only one hot-rodding around here."

"There are more footprints, too," Bess said, hurrying over to the second set of tracks. "They're pretty big, larger than George's. Maybe a guy's?"

Nancy studied them, then nodded. "Definitely. And with pointed toes and thick heels."

"Cowboy boots," Bess supplied.

"That's right. There *was* another car," George said slowly. "I remember seeing the lights come down the drive as I was leaving."

"Did you see the car or the driver?" Nancy asked, feeling a surge of excitement.

George shook her head. "Sorry. I was so busy being mad at Scooter, I didn't even glance at it."

"Whoever it was left in a hurry," Nancy said. She traced the second set of tire tracks with her eyes—a slip-sliding arc that skidded around where Scooter's car had parked, then curved dangerously close to the boathouse before heading back toward the drive.

Walking over to the boathouse, Nancy fingered a freshly splintered dent in the wood. "Look! The car hit here. The rear right fender, judging by those fishtail marks."

"There's some paint, too," Bess put in. "Bright red."

"So, we're looking for someone, probably a guy, who drives a red car and wears cowboy boots." George hesitated. "There must be lots of students at Wilder who fit that description."

"True. It's not like we can go chasing down every red car we see and accuse the driver of breaking Scooter's hand," Bess said.

George grimaced, shaking her head slowly. "Not if we want to find the person before we graduate."

"It's not that bad," Nancy insisted. "We already know of one person who has a possible motive. Vic Margolis." She went on to tell George and Bess about Vic becoming starting quarterback.

"You think he might have hurt Scooter to get his big chance?" George said, letting out a low whistle. "Sounds pretty whacked-out."

"No more than the story Scooter's been floating about you," Bess pointed out. "Let's face it, the whole situation is crazy."

"I guess," George said with a shrug. She started to turn away, then caught herself. "Wait. There's something else, too. The other day Jamal went off on a rampage about Scooter. It's probably nothing, but—"

At the mention of Pam's boyfriend, a signal went off in Nancy's mind. "Maybe it's not nothing," she said slowly. "I saw him at the game yesterday, taking an envelope from a guy wearing a Brockton football jacket."

"What would a guy from Brockton be doing at a game between Wilder and Rollins?" Bess questioned. "You mean Jamal was taking a secret payoff or something?" She sucked in her breath. "Are you saying that you think someone from Brockton paid him to break Scooter's hand?"

"I don't see it," George said with a frown. "Jamal's a decent guy. Maybe he's going through a hard time."

"You should at least talk to Pam about it," Nancy said. "You can't afford not to, George."

CHAPTER 9

George stood at the edge of the mall and stared at Beta house. The front lawn was a mess of mud, grass, and empty cans and bottles. Even from there, she could smell the stale beer.

Bess and Nancy had offered to come with her, but confronting Scooter was something George wanted to do on her own. She headed across the lawn and up the muddy stairs. The front door was propped open, and a few of the frat brothers were inside cleaning up.

"Where's Scooter?" George asked, stepping into the foyer.

She should have realized she wouldn't get a straight answer. The guys just stared at her. One of them was about seven feet tall, with so many muscles George was surprised he could even move. "Aren't you George? Look, Scooter doesn't want to see you."

"I'll bet," she said. The guy moved to block

her path, but George darted past him and took the stairs two at a time. She flew down the hallway, stopping at the third door on the right. It was slightly ajar, so she pushed it open and went in.

Scooter was sitting at his desk with his back to her. His left hand, covered by a plaster cast, rested on the desktop.

"Why did you do it?" George asked, coming up behind him. "Why'd you lie and tell everyone . . ."

Her voice broke off when she saw the three notes spread on the desk in front of Scooter. "Throw the big game with Brockton and you will score big money," read one of the notes. Another said, "Lose to the Cougars—or your luck will run out."

Before she could get a look at the third note, Scooter blinked, as if he had only just become aware that someone else was there. "Hey!" With lightning speed, he snatched the notes from his desktop and shoved them into a drawer. He winced in pain, then shot George an annoyed glance.

"What are you doing here?" he asked. "Did you come back to break my other hand?"

"You know that's not true," George shot back. "What's going on, Scooter? Did someone break your hand because of those?" she asked, pointing to the drawer where he'd stashed the notes. "Someone wanted you to throw the game with Brockton, didn't they?"

She was amazed by the intense, desperate look of fear that flashed in Scooter's eyes. Then, just as quickly, it was gone. "Haven't you harassed me enough?" he asked. "Breaking my hand? Stealing my rabbit's foot?"

George couldn't believe he had the nerve to lie like this while he was looking her straight in the eye. "You know I didn't do those things!"

"I should have taken everyone's advice and turned you in to campus security," he went on, as if he hadn't heard her.

"We both know why you didn't," George shot back. "Because you're afraid they'd find out what really happened. Why are you covering up? You know who broke your hand, and you know it's not me!"

She must have been shouting because a second later a voice from the doorway said, "Everything okay in here?"

George turned to see the big guy from downstairs. Two other brothers were standing right behind him. They all looked as if they were ready to jump in if they had to.

"Nothing I can't handle, Jimbo," Scooter said smoothly. He flicked a thumb at George. "She can't seem to get it through her thick head that I'm not interested."

"You liar!" George burst out before she could stop herself. She knew her face was bright red, and she could feel it get hotter when the three guys in the doorway started imitating her in falsetto voices.

"Forget it!" she muttered. "I should have known that you guys would stick together. Why would you be interested in something as trivial as the truth!"

Turning on her heel, she pushed past the guys and ran down the stairs. Even after she was out the door, she could hear their jeers and catcalls echoing behind her.

Well, that was productive, she thought, trying to calm down. Next time I want to have my character assassinated, I know exactly where to go.

Obviously she'd been wrong to think that Scooter would admit that he'd been lying once she saw him face-to-face.

So now what was she going to do?

"Sorry, I guess I'm distracted." Bess forced a smile and looked at the girl sitting next to her in the Kappa living room. "What did you say?"

She probably should have skipped that day's open house. It was almost impossible to concentrate on impressing the Kappas when she was so worried about George. But George had insisted on talking to Scooter on her own, so here Bess was.

"I was just saying that if you get a part in *Grease!*, we'll be seeing a lot of each other. I'm working on costumes." As the girl went on, Bess smiled politely. Suddenly the play didn't seem nearly as important as it had the day before. But she didn't want the Kappas to think she wasn't interested.

"Are you a drama major?" Bess asked. She tried to remember what the girl's name was. Laura or Lola or—

"Hi, Leila," Holly Thornton interrupted, coming up to them. "Hi, Bess. Glad you could make it."

Leila! That was it. Smiling at Holly, Bess said, "I promised, didn't I?"

"Speaking of drama," Holly went on, lowering her voice theatrically, "did you hear what happened to Scott Berenson?"

Bess frowned. "Yes," she said, gripping her cup more tightly, "but—"

"Lots of kids are talking about it," said a blond-haired girl Bess had seen at the sorority on Friday. "Can you believe what that girl did to him?"

Within seconds it seemed as if most of the girls in the room had joined in the conversation. Comments came flying from all directions. "What kind of person would do something like that?" "Someone with a pretty mean temper." "I know what she deserves, but it's not something I can say in public."

Bess just sat there, feeling her face grow hotter and hotter. After a few minutes she felt someone touch her arm and turned to find Soozie Beckerman there.

Oh, great. Just what I need.

"What do you think, Bess?" Soozie asked.

Bess had the feeling that there was a right answer and a wrong one, and that whatever she said was bound to be wrong.

She took a deep breath and put down her tea cup. "Do any of you people even know George Fayne?" she asked.

Several girls shook their heads. "What's the big deal, Bess?" Leila asked.

"How can you say all that stuff about someone you've never even met?" Bess went on. "If any of you actually knew George, you'd know that she didn't break Scooter Berenson's hand."

Everyone in the room was staring at her as if she'd completely lost her mind. "What makes you so sure?" Holly asked. "I mean, a friend of mine heard about it from Scooter himself."

The way she said it, Bess could tell Holly had already made up her mind that George was guilty. Everyone had.

"George happens to be my cousin, that's what makes me so sure," Bess shot back. Very slowly she got to her feet. "If all of you are so quick to judge her, without knowing any of the facts or even listening to George's side of the story"— she took a deep breath and dropped her napkin next to her tea cup—"then Kappa is definitely not the place for me."

Bess tried not to look at anyone, but just before she walked out the front door, she caught the expression on Soozie's face.

A satisfied, gloating smirk.

*   *   *

George tilted her face up to catch the afternoon rays as she walked back to Jamison Hall from Beta house. Indian summer, she thought. It couldn't make her forget about how completely ridiculous her life was right now, but it helped.

"There she is." A low voice made her look down again. A few feet away a group of kids were heading her way. George wasn't sure, but she thought they'd been at the Beta party.

Here we go again. The whispers—the looks. Very mature.

"Welcome to my life," she said under her breath. When it came to her word against Scooter's, it was obvious that most people would side with him. So much for honesty winning out.

At least one thing was starting to make more sense. After seeing the notes in Scooter's room, she at least knew why his hand had been broken. Nancy was going to flip when she found out that her hunch about gambling was right and that someone at Wilder was fixing games.

But who? she wondered. Vic Margolis? They definitely had to follow up on him, find out what he knew.

George let out a sigh as she headed into the dorm. And I have to talk to Pam about Jamal.

When she got to her room, Pam was sitting at her desk with her Western Civ text open in front of her. "Hi," she said, turning to smile at George. "Did you have any luck at the boathouse?"

"Sort of." George quickly filled her in on the second set of tire tracks and her confrontation with Scooter. "He wouldn't admit anything, though. About being threatened or about who really broke his hand."

"Game fixing, huh?" Pam said. "Whoever's behind it must be pretty serious. If he broke Scooter's hand, he could be capable of a lot worse. No wonder Scooter's not talking."

"Mmm." George lay down on her bed and crossed her hands under her head. "So, what did you and Jamal do after the game yesterday?" she asked, trying to keep her voice light.

"We didn't get together," Pam told her. "Jamal had something else to do."

"Something else?" George echoed. She'd been hoping that Pam could provide an alibi for her boyfriend. This was more problematic now. "Did he say what?"

"No. Why?" she asked suspiciously. "Hey, you're not trying to say that he's messed up with this gambling thing, are you?"

"Not necessarily. Probably not," George said quickly. "I have to check out every possibility, that's all."

Before Pam could object, George told her about Nancy's seeing Jamal take something from one of the Brockton Cougars. "You heard the way Jamal talked about Scooter," George finished. "He hates him."

"He was just wrung out from working so

much," Pam said defensively. "He'd never actually do anything." She shook her head, letting out her breath in an annoyed rush. "I don't believe you. Here I've been trying to help you out, and you come around accusing my boyfriend?"

"Sorry," George said truthfully. "It's just—"

"Forget it," Pam cut her off. "For your information, Jamal's car is white, not red. And he wouldn't be caught dead in cowboy boots. I know how badly you want to clear yourself, but you'd better go find yourself another bad guy," she said hotly, "because Jamal's not it!"

I hope not, George thought. I really hope not.

"Sunday afternoon at Java Joe's," Will murmured. He stood inside the entrance and scanned the coffee bar. "Why didn't I think of coming here sooner?"

The place smelled like mocha nut special brew, and it was filled with kids who looked as if they'd been sitting there for hours. Walking through the doors was like stepping through a time warp to a place where classes and exams and term papers didn't exist.

After spending most of the day staring at the walls of his apartment, it was exactly the kind of place he needed to be right then.

You might as well get it over with and call her, he told himself. He dropped his backpack at an empty table and headed for the phones in the back, next to the rest rooms.

Will still wasn't sure that going through with the date with George was the right thing. But Andy had lobbied pretty strongly in George's favor. In the end, Will decided that he should at least give her the chance to explain.

Which means that I'm either a very understanding guy—or a total sucker.

"Apparently, she wouldn't take no for an answer." A girl's voice at one of the rear tables caught Will's attention. He fished some change out of his pocket, listening idly to the conversation.

"She kidnapped Scooter in his own car and drove him down to the lake," the girl continued.

Will chuckled to himself as he looked up George's number. It sounded as if things had gotten even crazier than usual at the Beta party.

"She broke his hand?" the other girl at the table asked. "Who was it?"

Will was just popping his change into the coin slot when the first girl answered.

"Her name is weird," the girl said. "I mean, come on, a *girl* named George?"

Will stood frozen with his hand on the telephone's buttons. Oh, no, he thought. Don't tell me . . .

"But that's her name," the girl went on. "George Fayne."

"Let me do the talking, okay, George?" Pam said.

George nodded, then looked through the front window of the Bumblebee Diner. She knew that a lot of students from Wilder hung out there, but this was the first time she'd been there. She caught sight of a counter, booths, and jukebox. Jamal was sitting at a booth near the back, underneath a 1950s-style neon clock.

Pam had insisted that George have lunch with her and Jamal, so they could prove once and for all that he couldn't have been the one who'd broken Scooter's hand. George wasn't sure what she hoped would happen here. If Jamal had attacked Scooter, that would at least clear her name. But what would it do to her friendship with Pam?

"Hi, Jamal." Pam leaned into the booth where her boyfriend was sitting and kissed him. "You don't mind if George eats with us, do you?" she asked.

"No problem." Jamal scooted over to make room for Pam, while George slid in opposite them. "What's up, George?" he said, giving her a wide smile. "Sorry I was a little rough the other day. I've been stressed out lately."

"There's a lot of that going around," George said with a halfhearted laugh.

The waitress showed up to take their order, and they all ordered burgers and fries. George had been so preoccupied with finding out the truth about Scooter that she hadn't realized how hungry she was.

"So, how come you're in such a good mood

all of a sudden?" Pam asked Jamal after their waitress left. "You must have been having some good time last night without me."

"Without you? Never," he joked. He did seem less uptight than he had on Friday, George thought. Was that because his money problems were eased, thanks to being paid for hurting Scooter?

"What'd you do?" Pam pressed.

Jamal frowned. "This and that," he answered vaguely. "I don't remember exactly."

This and that? It wasn't the most direct answer George had ever heard. She could tell that Pam was wondering why Jamal was being evasive, too.

"You have some new friends you're hiding from me or something?" Pam asked.

Just then the waitress arrived with their drinks, and George took a sip of her Coke. "Didn't I see you talking to a guy from Brockton at the Chargers game yesterday afternoon?" Actually, Nancy had seen him, but Jamal didn't have to know that.

"Who are you, the secret police?" Jamal asked, annoyed.

"I just noticed the guy giving you something, that's all," George said quickly. "Sorry I mentioned it."

Jamal's eyes flitted back and forth between Pam and George. "Look, that was nothing," he finally said. "Just a friend of mine who owed me some money. Now can we please drop the interrogation and eat?"

He smiled when he said it, but George noticed the nervous way his dark eyes kept darting around the diner as if there was something he wasn't telling them.

Sooner or later, she thought, I'm going to find out what it is.

Nancy hung up the pay phone outside the one-story brick building that housed Wilder University's campus security. As she moved away from the building, she slipped her hands into Kara's jacket pockets, then groaned when they caught in the frayed, split red fabric.

This was getting more than a little annoying, she thought. Here she'd bought a new leather jacket, and so far the only person to wear it was Kara. Still, after talking to George, Nancy was too preoccupied to give her roommate much thought.

"Game fixing?" she murmured out loud. George had told her all about the notes she'd seen in Scooter's room. Nancy was willing to bet that one of them was the same note she'd seen Scooter reading in the locker room on Friday. No wonder he'd been so spooked. Someone had threatened him.

Scooter must have refused to throw next week's game, Nancy reasoned. And that was why his hand had been broken. Whoever was trying to fix the game had obviously made good on his threat.

Not that I have a clue as to who the person is. Or any hard evidence to back up my theory.

Her trip to campus security had been a total bust. She hadn't expected to run into any problems getting a list of red cars on campus. But the officer she'd spoken to wouldn't even give her the time of day. Sorry, he'd told her. That's confidential information. Even after she'd explained what the problem was, he wouldn't budge. At times like this, Nancy really missed River Heights. Chief McGinnis would have given her that list, no doubt about it.

But he's known you your whole life, she reminded herself. Here at Wilder, people like that officer or even Gail Gardeski weren't going to just take her word for things. She had to prove herself.

Nancy was still deep in thought when she reached Thayer Hall. She was just pulling open the glass doors when she heard the screech of tires peeling around the drive leading up to the dorm. A second later a bright red Fiero stopped in front of her.

"Nancy! Hi," Kara called, waving from the passenger seat. Next to her, Vic was sitting behind the wheel.

Hmm, thought Nancy. Vic Margolis—red car— And the quick, suspicious look Vic gave her. What's that all about? Don't tell me my luck in this case is actually changing.

"Hi, Kara, Vic," Nancy said, trying to keep her voice casual. "How's everything?"

"Great!" Kara said. She bubbled on about sororities or something, but Nancy wasn't really listening. She sauntered closer to the sports car.

There was no missing the dent, or the scratched paint, just above the right rear fender.

Vic Margolis had just become her top suspect.

CHAPTER 10

"**W**hat planet are you on?" Kara's voice broke into Nancy's thoughts.

"Hmm?" Nancy saw that Kara had gotten out of the car and was staring at her expectantly. "Sorry. Did you say something?"

Kara rolled her eyes. "And some people call me flaky. Come on," she said, pointing a finger toward her neck. "Tell me this isn't the most gorgeous thing you've ever seen."

Nancy's gaze settled on her own leather jacket, which Kara was still wearing, of course. "You're right. That jacket is beautiful. Where'd you get it?" she asked. But if Kara noticed the sarcasm in her voice, she didn't let on.

"I was talking about my new necklace!" she said, grinning from ear to ear. "Vic gave it to me."

Nancy did a double take when she finally noticed the thick gold chain and charm around

Kara's neck. They were elegant—and very expensive looking.

"Gorgeous is an understatement," she commented. She turned to Vic, who was taking his time getting out of the Fiero. "It must have cost a fortune."

Vic shot her an uncomfortable glance but didn't say anything.

"Vic doesn't worry about money," Kara put in lightly. "Anyway, I'm worth it."

Nancy decided to let that comment pass. "You must be psyched about starting against the Cougars this weekend," she said to Vic. "What a great opportunity for you."

"I'm ready for it," he said. His face was impassive, but his eyes started to show discomfort.

"No kidding!" Kara said, giving his arm a squeeze.

Ready enough to break Scooter's hand in order to be starting quarterback? "I guess there's a lot of pressure, too," Nancy went on blithely. "You know how carried away people get. I hear there's some big money riding on the game."

She watched Vic closely for his reaction, but he remained stone faced. "I've got to leave," he told Kara. He gave her a hasty kiss on the cheek before getting back into the Fiero. "See you."

As he sped down the drive, Nancy followed him with her eyes. Go ahead. Stick to your strong, silent act, she thought. It won't change anything.

I'm onto you, Vic.

* * *

Kara's good mood evaporated as quickly as her boyfriend's car made it down the drive.

"What are you trying to do, Nancy?" she asked, facing off with her roommate. "Vic and I have a really good energy going between us now. Why did you have to wreck it with all those questions?"

Nancy blinked before turning back to her. "Does Vic wear cowboy boots?" she asked.

Kara just stared at her. Nancy hadn't heard a word she'd said. "What if he does? What does that have to do with anything?"

"I'm pretty sure that the person who broke Scooter's hand drives a red car," Nancy told her. "George, Bess, and I went to the boathouse and . . ."

For the next ten minutes Nancy went on with an endless list of so-called evidence. Dents, paint scratches, footprints. It was so factual and dry. Kara could hardly make herself pay attention.

"You're so cynical," she said when Nancy was finally done. "Personally, I think you would be a happier person if you stopped thinking so much and started paying more attention to your feelings."

"Well, my gut feeling is that Vic is hiding something," Nancy told her. "Do you know what it is?"

"Why do you have to be so suspicious?" Kara asked, exasperated. "Vic would never do the things you're talking about. I mean, throw a game? Break someone's hand?" She fingered her gold chain, then shook her head adamantly. "Scooter's a friend of his. He just wouldn't do it."

The look Nancy gave her told Kara that she hadn't completely believed the message.

"Kara, if Vic is up to something, and I'm not sure that he is," Nancy said, "but if he is, wouldn't you want to know about it?"

"Having a red car and cowboy boots doesn't make him a criminal," Kara insisted.

"Okay, okay," Nancy said, holding up her hands.

At least she was finally letting it drop. But Vic was already gone, and Kara's mood was shot. As Nancy headed inside the dorm, Kara thought over the whole ridiculous conversation.

Vic would never do the things Nancy suspected. And if he'd been acting kind of distant lately, Kara was sure he'd come out of it soon.

At least, she hoped so.

Peter sighted down the length of his cue stick, judging the angle on his next shot. After being holed up with his biochem book all day, he needed a break from studying.

Who are you kidding? You know what you're really trying to escape from, and it isn't studying.

He hadn't been able to stop thinking about Nancy and Dawn and how messed up he was about them both. He'd spent three years running from his past, but he couldn't seem to get completely clear of it.

"Peter Goodwin." Stephanie Keats's sugar-sweet voice came from somewhere to the right. "Imagine running into you down here. What a coincidence."

"Mmm," he murmured, his eyes still on the cue ball. Lately she'd been showing up everywhere he happened to be—at Java Joe's, down here in the Thayer Hall Tombs. He was starting to get the feeling that coincidence had nothing to do with their meetings.

With a sure stroke of his stick, Peter sent the cue ball spinning into the nine ball, a perfect bank shot to the corner. When he straightened up and looked at Stephanie, the first thing he noticed was the hungry gleam in her eye—the look of a tiger on the prowl.

"Bravo," she said, sidling up to him. "But then, you seem to excel at everything."

Except relationships. Pushing the thought from his mind, Peter gave a halfhearted smile and said, "If you say so." He moved around the table to sight his next shot.

"I was thinking," Stephanie said. "Gray Zone is playing at the student center on Saturday. Feel like going?"

Peter started to say no, but then he caught himself. Stephanie was nice enough, and he could use a friend right now.

"Sure," he said with a sigh. Then he straightened up and turned and gave her a smile. "Sounds good."

*   *   *

Nancy was still thinking about Vic when she got to her room. It was looking more and more as if he was the person who broke Scooter's hand. But was he behind the game fixing, too? Or did someone else pay Vic to break Scooter's hand and throw the big game?

Taking off Kara's short red jacket, Nancy dropped it on her bed, then stared idly at the books on her desk. "If I could only find a way to—"

She blinked, staring at the matchbook that stuck out from beneath her journalism text. "Of course!" she said, picking it up. She'd completely forgotten about the phone number she'd gotten from Ryan, the guy she'd overheard talking to the bookie.

Nancy took a deep breath, going over everything she knew so far. There was a bookie on campus, someone who'd threatened to hurt Ryan. It made sense that if students were betting, they'd be betting *for* Wilder. After all, the Norsemen were number one in the conference this season. If the bookie could find a way to make sure that Wilder lost, he'd cash in big-time.

The phone jangled in the background, but Nancy was concentrating so hard that she didn't pick it up right away. Her theory made sense. Every instinct in her body told her she was on the right track.

It wasn't until the third ring that she finally answered. "Hello?"

"Hi. It's me."

The deep voice hit her like a ton of bricks. "Ned—" She was so stunned, she didn't know what to say.

"I just wanted to apologize for the way I left. I was a class-A jerk for taking off without saying goodbye," he said. "Sorry."

Two days after the fact, she thought. But at least he'd called.

"I guess I deserve the silent treatment," he said after a moment. "I just figured there wasn't anything left to say, so why stick around."

To say goodbye? To let me know that what we had together wasn't just a figment of my imagination? That it was special to you, too? But somehow, Nancy couldn't bring herself to say these things to Ned.

"Well, I'm glad you made it back to Emerson okay," she told him.

"Listen, Nancy. I said a lot of things the other night. I just want you to know . . ."

He sounded so sad and distant. It made her heart ache. "Yes?"

"I know you'd never cheat on me," he said. She could hear him taking a deep breath. "I guess blaming you was easier than recognizing that things just aren't the same anymore. For both of us."

That was the understatement of the year. "No, they aren't," she agreed. "So"—Nancy took a deep breath—"I don't want to sound like a cliché or anything, but do you think we can still be friends?"

"Wow. There's a concept," Ned said, laughing.
She smiled despite herself. "Well?"

"I think you know the answer," he said softly.
"Just because we're not seeing each other anymore doesn't mean we have to be strangers."

When Nancy hung up the phone a few minutes
later, she felt better about Ned than she had in
weeks. Friends. It felt right to think about him
that way. To think about them both moving on.

"Speaking of which . . ."

Nancy picked up the matchbook cover again
and stared at the scrawled phone number Ryan
had given her. It was her ticket to finding out
whether it was Vic, or someone else, who was
behind the game fixing. And it had been right
under her nose since Friday.

"Well, better late than never," she murmured.
Clutching the scrap of paper, she picked up her
phone again and punched in the number.

The young man gave a satisfied smirk as he
hung up the phone. He'd recognized her voice,
all right. And he'd said all the right things, pre-
tending to go along with her bogus story about
wanting to bet fifty dollars on the Brockton
game.

You think you're smart, Nancy Drew, he
thought, fingering Scooter's rabbit's foot. But
you'll find out soon enough that you can't out-
maneuver me.

Ordinarily, the hired help handled all of the

money transactions. After all, it wasn't smart business to make yourself too vulnerable.

But this was one transaction he was going to take care of himself.

Great plan, Drew. Going to a deserted lake in the dead of night. She wasn't crazy about the spot the bookie had chosen for her to drop off her bet money—beneath the bench at the lake overlook. But it wasn't as if she had a choice. The guy she'd spoken with had made it clear that until he could trust her, she had to play by his rules. No meeting face-to-face, no giving her the P.O. box number where people usually sent the money they were betting.

"How do I know I can trust you?" she'd asked.

"Because you don't have any choice" had been the answer. The mysterious, almost mocking way he'd said it hadn't exactly reassured her.

"I hope I'm not making a huge mistake," she murmured.

The sound of her voice hung eerily in the still night air. She'd left the lights of the boathouse behind her and was already almost halfway around the lake. So far, she hadn't run into a single person. No one was crazy enough to be out here in the pitch-black night.

No one except me.

Hitting the button to illuminate the digital numbers on her watch, she saw that it was a quarter to eleven. She had fifteen minutes to leave her fifty dollars. The instructions had been clear:

drop the money and leave. But she didn't see how the bookie would be able to spot one very inconspicuous person hiding in the woods nearby.

"Whoa!" Nancy stumbled as her foot caught on a root, but she managed to steady herself by grabbing a low-hanging branch. Even though her eyes had adjusted fairly well to the darkness, the path was still just murky blackness beneath her feet.

A few moments later she saw the overlook, a small spit of land that jutted out into the water. A bench of rough-hewn logs sat there. Taking the paper bag with her fifty dollars in it, Nancy placed it beneath the bench. For a full minute she stood still and listened, but all she heard was the rustle of wind in the trees and the single hoot of an owl.

The coast is clear, she decided. Moving as quietly as she could, she stepped off the path and crouched behind a thick bush about ten yards away. From there, she had a clear view of the bench. She was sure no one would be able to spot her. Her senses on red alert, she settled back and waited.

Lake Winneshobe at night was a truly awesome sight. A sliver of a crescent moon peeked out from behind the evergreens that ringed the lake, sending a silvery wash over the water. It was unbelievably romantic. Nancy couldn't help wishing that someone was there to share it with her.

She automatically pictured Ned's gorgeous

square-cut face, could practically feel his strong arms around her.

The crashing sounds of footsteps jolted Nancy from her thoughts. She was expecting to see someone in front of her, picking up the money. But what was he doing behind her? Something was terribly, terribly wrong here.

She whirled around, staring frantically into the dense woods. She couldn't see anyone, but she could hear the person heading her way—and fast!

The realization hit her with hurricane force—I'm being followed!

Peter was lost in thought as he walked around Lake Winneshobe. He knew campus security didn't like students hanging out in deserted parts of the campus at night. Not that he'd planned on coming this far. He'd just gone out for some fresh air to clear his head. The next thing he knew he was on the lake path. It was as if his body had switched to automatic pilot.

A sudden noise from among the trees caught his attention. Whoa! That wasn't just a raccoon or a chipmunk. It sounded like Bigfoot!

Peter stopped walking and stared into the shadowy black trees. "Hello? Who's—"

A dark shape streaked out from the trees, heading straight for him. A person, he realized. He blinked as the faintest glow of moonlight lit up the person's face.

"Nancy! What are you—"

A split second later she slammed into him,

knocking the breath out of him. They both went flying. The next thing Peter knew, they were splashing into the lake in a tangle of arms and legs.

The icy water sent his whole body into shock. As his head went under, he felt frantically for Nancy while trying to right himself. Finally his feet found the muddy bottom and his hand found her arm. When he pushed his head back up and opened his eyes, Nancy was clinging to him, her face just inches from his.

"Peter!" she said, gasping for air. "I'm so— glad—to—see you . . ." Her teeth were chattering and her hair was a soaking, matted mess. Even in the darkness, the look in her eyes was so beautiful and scared and vulnerable. Before he could stop himself, he gave in to the urge that had become stronger and stronger lately.

He kissed her.

Nancy closed her eyes and surrendered herself to the sweetness of Peter's kiss. She was hardly aware of what was happening, where they were. All she knew was that it felt deliciously wonderful to be this close to him.

"I'm sorry." Peter stepped awkwardly away from her, then stumbled in the waist-high water.

Nancy grabbed his arm, and again he was so close that she could feel the amazing electricity. "It's all m-my fault," she murmured. Her mind was whirling. What had just happened?

"No. It's just that, I shouldn't have, that's all."

Peter couldn't quite meet her gaze. He turned away from her and waded toward dry ground. Sensing his awkwardness, Nancy suddenly felt cold and wet and very self-conscious.

"We're b-both getting over r-relationships," she stammered, rubbing her freezing cold arms as she waded out of the water after him. She was babbling, thinking about everything at once—Ned, Peter's kiss, and . . .

Something much scarier. "P-Peter, someone was chasing me."

He stopped and turned to her, his face filled with concern. "Are you serious?"

She nodded. The shock of running into him had made her forget about her attacker for a minute, but now she stared grimly into the darkened trees. When she didn't hear anything, she said, "He must have left when he heard you."

"Who was it? What are you doing out here, anyway?" Peter asked.

"I was—" She clamped her mouth shut just in time. Game fixing was serious business. People were getting hurt. Until she knew who was behind it, she couldn't talk about it to anyone. "I left something out here earlier today that I really needed for the school paper," she lied smoothly.

Peter was looking at her as if she'd suddenly grown a second head. "So you decided to get it in the middle of the night, by yourself? Wouldn't it make more sense to wait until morning?"

How are you going to explain that one, Nancy?

"You know how journalists are," she said.

125

"Working day and night, searching for the untold story and all that." She tried to laugh, but her teeth were chattering too much. "I guess I got carried away."

Peter raised an eyebrow at her, rubbing the soaking wet sleeves of his shirt. "Yeah," he said.

"Now that I think of it, there probably wasn't anyone following me," she went on quickly. Cut him off at the pass, before he can think too much about how lame your story is. "I must have been spooked."

As she spoke, Nancy walked back to the overlook. Bending low, she saw that the paper bag she'd left was still there. "Here it is," she said brightly, reaching under the bench to pull it out.

She shot a quick look inside the bag, then did a double take. Weird. The guy hadn't even bothered to take the fifty dollars.

Then it hit her. Whoever had chased her didn't even care about the money. All he cared about was getting her.

CHAPTER 11

George braced herself as she stepped into the boathouse for crew practice on Monday morning. It was before six, but about twenty women were there already. As soon as they saw George, a buzz of hushed whispers shot through the group.

Stifling a sigh, George went over to the group and leaned against the wall. Wilder was a big place. Not everyone was obsessed with football and the frat scene. She'd had to put up with some glares and whispered comments around campus since Saturday night. But that was nothing compared to this. If they didn't have assigned positions for crew practice, George was sure that her shell would be deserted.

"She's got a lot of nerve, showing up," one girl whispered.

George ignored her, but inside she was burning. It's not fair! she wanted to scream. I didn't do anything. But she knew it wouldn't do any good to try to explain.

She turned as someone else entered the boathouse. This time, at least it was someone she knew. "Hi, Eileen," she said, greeting Nancy's suitemate. "How's it going?"

Eileen's friendly expression disappeared when she saw George. "Not bad," she mumbled. Then she walked right past George and started talking to one of the other girls.

Gee, it's great to see you, too, George thought dryly.

"I'm in her shell, too," someone was saying to Eileen. "Talk about bad luck!"

"If I'd known she was going to be here," another girl said, "I would have skipped practice and finished the reading for environmental science."

Hearing that, George's stomach twisted into an even tighter knot. Environmental science was her first class, too.

And Will's.

I can't face him, she thought. No way.

His voice had been so cold and mechanical when he'd called to break their date the day before. He hadn't said a word about Scooter or the rumors that she'd broken his hand, but his voice told her all that she needed to know.

He hates me.

Stephanie turned off her hair blower and set it on the metal counter that ran above the three sinks in the suite's bathroom. Thanks to the right amount of gel and styling, her dark hair looked perfect—slightly tousled yet elegant.

With a critical eye, she surveyed the makeup next to her hair blower. She wasn't afraid to accentuate her finer features, just the right amount of blush to bring out her high cheekbones, a little kohl around her eyes for exotic appeal, and the usual red on her lips.

She turned as the bathroom door opened, then raised one eyebrow when she saw Nancy. *Hmm,* she thought. *Nancy looks positively bleary eyed this morning. This could be fun.*

Casually, Stephanie began putting her cosmetics back in her cloth bag. "Pulling an all-nighter so early in the semester?" she asked. Then she added quickly, "Never mind. Of course you are. Always prepared."

Nancy barely glanced at her as she hung her towel next to the sink and began to wash her face.

Not good enough, thought Stephanie. She'd put a lot of effort into looking this good. Nancy could at least have the courtesy to be jealous.

Stephanie clicked her tongue, giving Nancy the slow once-over. "You should really do something about those circles, Nancy," she said. "And that washed-out complexion. Everyone needs her beauty rest."

"Thanks for your concern. I'll keep that in mind," Nancy mumbled, shooting Stephanie an annoyed glance. She splashed some more water on her face, then reached for her towel.

"Then again, now that you and Ned aren't seeing each other anymore," Stephanie went on blithely, "I suppose you don't really care how you look."

Before Nancy could say anything, Stephanie moved in with the clincher. "That's a luxury those of us with love lives can't afford. I mean, imagine if I looked like you when I meet Peter for our date on Saturday night."

She saw the surprise and hurt in Nancy's eyes. Score! Stephanie thought smugly.

"Well, see you," she told Nancy. Tucking her cosmetics bag under her arm, she walked slowly from the bathroom.

"Well, here goes," George murmured aloud as she pulled open the doors to the science building. "Just try not to self-destruct when you see him, okay?"

She had decided not to cut environmental science. After all, she didn't want to jeopardize her grade, especially when she hadn't done anything wrong. Besides, she was going to have to face Will sometime.

George tried to act cool, but she couldn't keep her eyes from darting around, searching out Will's familiar tall figure. She had to make herself breathe normally while she walked up to the second floor and headed down the hall to the environmental science classroom.

Then, out of the corner of her eye, she saw him. He was leaning against the wall a few feet from her, wearing a flannel shirt and jeans. George felt an intense surge of emotion.

She didn't realize that she'd stopped walking, but suddenly her eyes locked on Will's. Anger, hurt, and bitterness all flashed across his face so quickly that she wasn't even sure she'd seen them. Then Will looked down and shook his head.

"What a joke," he muttered. "I can't believe I actually thought there was something special about you."

George stared at him. For a moment she couldn't move or think, so many deep emotions were churning inside of her. Then, suddenly, everything she'd been holding inside for the past two days came tumbling out.

"Don't you think you're being just a little unfair?" she asked. She strode over to Will and faced him squarely. "You don't know anything about what happened, and here you are, judging me like everyone else!"

Will blinked and looked as if he was about to say something, but George couldn't stop the torrent of words from rushing out of her mouth.

"I mean, you know me, Will. So maybe I made a mistake by going to that Beta party with Scooter."

"You got that right," he muttered, but George wasn't about to let him turn things around on her.

"And I definitely should have been more honest with you about it," she went on. "But do you really think I'd do something like break Scooter's hand?"

The more she said, the angrier she felt. Will was just standing there with his hands in his pockets. Why didn't he do something? Or say something? But he just stared at her, his dark eyes flashing with uncertainty.

"I don't suppose it ever occurred to you that I could use the support of my friends right now." George shook her head bitterly. "Obviously, I was wrong to think that's what you are."

This time she didn't wait for a reaction. Clutching her books in a death-grip, she turned away from him. For the first time she noticed the group of students standing outside their classroom. They were all staring at her and Will, but she didn't care. She'd meant every word.

Stepping past them, she walked into her classroom and sat down.

"Gail?" Nancy stepped across the cluttered office of the campus newspaper. Typeset galleys of that week's edition of *Wilder Times* were spread out on tables and even on the floor, with students proofreading them.

"Hmm?" Gail answered, not looking up from the galley she was proofing. She was sitting at a desk, piled high with papers. A bulletin board on the wall next to her had still more papers tacked to it, along with a calendar with press dates marked in red.

"About my interview?" Nancy asked. "I was wondering if you'd had a chance to read it."

Gail reached into the high stack in front of her and pulled two sheets from it. "Got it right here. Strong first effort, all in all," she said, handing Nancy both pages. "This one's your interview with Scooter. That other is the rewrite I did."

"Rewrite?" Nancy asked, frowning. She'd been hoping to do any revisions herself.

Gail nodded. "Had to. Otherwise we wouldn't have been able to get the piece into tomorrow's paper," she told Nancy.

She didn't say anything about Nancy's missed deadline, but Nancy got the message: If she'd gotten the article in on time, she might have had the chance to rewrite it on her own. Squelching her disappointment, Nancy just said, "I understand."

She walked slowly away, scanning the rewrite. Gail had shortened a lot of her sentences. And the way she'd restructured the opening paragraph did make it much clearer.

"Keep two things in mind," Gail called out to her. "Never use a ten-cent word where a nickel word will do," she said. "And make sure you've got all your facts straight."

Nancy blinked, remembering what Gail had said about getting hard proof of gambling on campus. She turned and went back to the editor-in-chief's desk. "I was wondering if you'd reconsider doing the story we talked about," she said, keeping her voice low. "The one on gambling. There are some new developments."

She started to tell Gail about her theory that Scooter's arm had been broken because he wouldn't go along with a plan to fix the big game with Brockton, but the editor-in-chief cut her off.

"I thought I already made myself clear on this," Gail said with an irritated sweep of her hand. "Proof. Cold, hard proof. That's what I need before I can consider doing any story, especially one as big as this." She gave Nancy a probing stare, then added, *"Wilder Times* is not a forum for getting your friends off the hook, you know."

Nancy's mouth fell open. "What! You actually think I would—"

"I never make assumptions," Gail put in quickly. "This girl, the one they say hurt Scooter. She's a friend of yours, right?" When Nancy nodded, the editor-in-chief said firmly, "You're too close. Personal involvement can make for irresponsible journalism."

Nancy opened her mouth to object, but Gail had already turned back to the galley she was proofing. "That's a final answer. I don't want to hear about it again."

"Fine," Nancy said, biting off the word. She spun around and headed for the door. Gail had all but accused her of making up the gambling story just to get George out of trouble. As if she'd resort to printing lies!

"Ooh!" Nancy seethed, storming down the

hallway toward the stairs. Gail may know journalism, she thought, but she definitely does not know me!

"So Gail thinks you're lying about the gambling?" George leaned back on her elbows on the grassy lawn next to the library, where she, Nancy, and Bess were studying. "That figures."

"She could have at least heard me out," Nancy said, twisting a blade of grass between her fingers. "I mean, we really are getting closer to finding out who's trying to fix Saturday's game with Brockton."

George could tell that Nancy was upset about being shut down on the story. "Besides which, you risked your life last night trying to find out who it is. What does she think, that someone followed you just because he didn't have anything better to do?" she asked. "You'd think Gail would realize that means you're onto something."

"I still can't believe that happened," Bess said. She looked up from the biology book in her lap, shivering. "I'm just glad you saw that guy Peter from your dorm, Nan."

Nancy just nodded, but George noticed the slight flush creep into her cheeks. This wasn't the first time she'd blushed when Peter Goodwin's name came up. Nancy wasn't the type to rush into anything, but George could tell there was something in the air between her and Peter.

"Gail's right about the proof, anyway," Nancy said. "We don't actually have the threatening notes George saw, so we can't prove Scooter received them."

"And some muddy car tracks and footprints that are already gone aren't exactly conclusive evidence that I didn't break his hand," George added. She gave a wry smile. "The way things are going, it'd probably be easier to prove that aliens are invading Earth."

"You mean they're not?" Bess asked. "I thought maybe they'd taken over Professor Ross's mind and that's why biology makes no sense whatsoever to me."

"Sorry, Bess. No such luck," Nancy said, laughing. "Anyway, even if we don't have all the answers, at least you got to tell Will off, George."

George nodded. She was glad that Bess and Nancy were around to back her up, but it still hurt to know that there wasn't any hope of fixing things between her and Will. Crossing her arms under her head, she looked up at the crisp, cloudless sky. "I can't talk about it anymore. It's too depressing."

She reached out to tap Bess's textbook. "I can't believe you're studying bio instead of rehearsing," she said. "Isn't your audition this afternoon?"

Bess nodded. "Brian and I have our parts down as much as we can," she said, her blue eyes gleaming. "We decided not to rehearse any more, so we'll be fresh for the actual audition." She groaned, flipping through the pages of her heavy text. "If biology doesn't kill me first, that is."

A shadow fell over Bess's book, and George looked up to see a blond guy with glasses standing next to them. "Hi, Bess. How's it going?"

"Don't ask. I don't understand a single word of this stuff. I might as well be reading Greek!" Bess told him, rolling her eyes. "Oh—by the way, this is Tom, you guys," she said to Nancy and George. "Tom, meet Nancy and George."

A smile played over Tom's mouth as he nodded hello. George had the feeling that he was checking them out.

"I could help you out," Tom offered, crouching down next to Bess. "I'm a physics major, but I did well in bio, too."

"Yeah?" Bess told him, but George could see her hesitate. "Um, maybe. I mean, I'm pretty busy right now. Could we leave it open?"

George caught the amused look Nancy gave her. Bess obviously didn't want anything to get in the way of whatever might happen between her and Brian.

"Sure," Tom said, but George noticed the way his eyebrows knit together into a slight frown. He scribbled a phone number in one of the notebooks he was carrying, then ripped out the paper and gave it to Bess. "Call me any time if you're up for a study session."

Tom stood up again, but George had the feeling that he wanted an excuse to linger. "Physics," she said, just to make conversation. "Sounds like a killer major."

Tom shrugged. "It's not bad, but the labs eat

up a lot of time. I was stuck in the science building all Saturday night while everyone else was partying."

Beats my Saturday night, George thought.

She was glad when Bess started talking about biology again and she could close her eyes and listen. What a relief to be thinking about someone else's problems for a change.

Bess gripped Brian's arm in the semidarkness of Hewlitt's theater. "Look at that stage. It's huge! I can't go up there." She moaned and sank her head into her hands. "Why did I let you talk me into auditioning?"

"Because you're a glutton for punishment. We all are," Brian told her. "It's a well-known fact. Why else would we choose to go up there and make complete idiots of ourselves, with all these people watching?"

"Thanks, Brian. You don't know how much better that makes me feel," Bess said weakly.

She felt her panic deepen as she glanced around the theater. This was her first college theatrical audition! Groups of kids were scattered among the seats and in the aisles. The director and his assistant were sitting front row center, calling out names one by one. It figured that they were auditioning for the chorus first. Any second now, all of these people were going to be watching her.

"Star alert!" Brian whispered, cutting into her thoughts. "Casey Fontaine just got here."

"Really?" She swiveled her head around until she spotted the tall, red-haired girl who was sitting in the back of the theater. Bess had been as awed as everyone else to learn that a TV star was starting her freshman year at Wilder. A buzz went through the theater until the director cleared his throat and asked for quiet.

"I heard she's trying out for a part," Brian whispered, hunching down in his seat next to Bess.

"As if she needs to. I mean, *The President's Daughter* was only the top-rated TV show for three seasons running," Bess said. "But Casey said she wants to audition just like the rest of us. She's not even trying for one of the leads."

Brian stared at her. "You talked to her? In person?"

"What can I say? I guess I have the kind of natural charm that attracts outrageously successful teen stars," Bess said, grinning. "That, plus I just happened to run into her when I checked the schedule in the drama department for the fifty zillionth time to make sure the audition time hadn't changed. She seems really nice."

"What about all the rumors?" Brian asked, glancing over his shoulder at Casey again. "You know, that her parents wanted her to leave L.A. because they were afraid she was getting too deep into the club scene there."

"Sex, drugs, and rock 'n' roll," Bess quipped.

"Sorry, but I didn't have time to get her entire life story. I only met her for two seconds."

"Kirsten Lowell!" the director called out.

"They're up to the *L*'s!" Bess felt her entire body tighten with fear. "Quick, do something to distract me before I pass out."

"Don't faint, okay?" he whispered. "It's dramatic, but you might score more brownie points if we were trying out for *Gone With the Wind* instead of *Grease!*" Brian started to laugh, but in the next instant his whole face changed.

"Brian? Are you okay?" Bess followed his gaze to the front of the theater, where half a dozen people were standing. "You look like you just saw a ghost. Did somebody beam down here from another dimension or something?"

"Could be," he murmured, his eyes still on the group. Then he blinked and turned to her with a smile. "Have I told you that you're the best friend I've ever had?"

"What does that have to do with—" Bess caught herself. Looking at the light in his green eyes, the slightly shy expression on his face, she knew it was about to happen. This was it. Brian was going to tell her how he really felt about her. "What's up, Brian? Are you about to get serious on me?" She nodded toward the stage, where Kirsten Lowell was still singing. "Now?"

"It's a now-or-never kind of thing," he said. "Sappy confessions aren't exactly my strong suit.

I mean, maybe you've already guessed that I have a crush on someone."

He was so cute when he was shy. Bess couldn't help grinning at him. "Yeah. I kind of got that impression," she told him.

"Well," Brian took a deep breath, raking a hand through his hair. "I want to show you who it is."

"Cool." Bess sat back and waited expectantly.

"It's someone from my drama class," he went on.

Bess felt all the excitement drain from her body. "Drama class? I didn't even get in to drama."

"That's not exactly a news flash, Bess," Brian said, giving her a confused glance.

He didn't get it. He wasn't even looking at her anymore. All of his attention was focused on the group near the stage, not on what she'd said. Bess couldn't bring herself to look at whoever it was he was nodding at.

He doesn't want you, her mind screamed. It's someone else.

"Marvin! Bess Marvin."

Bess blinked in panic. Not now, she thought. This can't be happening. It's a bad dream, and any second I'll wake up and go back to my real life.

"Bess Marvin!" the director called again. "Are you here?" He had stood up and was looking around the theater.

Uh-oh. This is my real life. Bess sank her head into her hands. If I could just have a minute—

"Right here!" Brian called out. He pulled her to her feet and whispered, "Good luck. It's show time!"

Bess started walking dazedly toward the stage. It's show time, all right. Horror show time.

CHAPTER 12

Nancy was in the lobby, waiting for the elevators after dinner on Monday night. The same questions had been running through her mind all day long. How was she going to find out who the bookmaker was? Somehow the person knew that she was a threat to him. But how? And how was she going to outsmart him?

Think like a criminal, she told herself. Shouldn't be too hard. After skipping some of her classes and assignments, she was starting to feel like one. Academically, at least.

Nancy looked up as the elevator doors slid open and she found herself face-to-face with Dawn. Dawn gave her a surprised glance as she stepped out into the lobby.

"I just about gave up looking for you," she told Nancy.

"Oh?" Nancy followed the RA as she stepped away from the elevators. It was the first time

Dawn had spoken to her since seeing her and Peter walking together on Saturday night.

"Yes. I went to see Julie at the rehab center this afternoon," Dawn said.

Julie Hammerman had been in Suite 301 for less than a week before her suitemates discovered that she had a serious drug problem. She'd gone on a stealing spree in the dorm, taking everything valuable that she could get her hands on and then selling it to support her habit. Nancy was glad Julie had agreed to get treatment in a nearby rehabilitation center.

"How's she doing?" she asked Dawn.

"She's a lot more stable and secure," Dawn said. "Her counselor thinks she might be ready to check out by the end of the semester."

"Great," Nancy said.

"Isn't it? Anyway, I thought you'd want to know." Dawn's gaze shifted uncomfortably, and she moved a few steps away from Nancy. "Well, I . . ."

"Look, about the other night, when you saw Peter and me," Nancy began. "I don't want you to think that—"

"You don't have to explain," Dawn cut in. She gave Nancy a halfhearted smile. "I know I overreacted. Just because he and I broke up doesn't mean you can't be friends with him."

Friends? Is that what we are? Nancy pushed aside the confused emotions that churned inside her whenever she thought about Peter. "I just don't want to cause any tension in the suite," she said truthfully.

"Me, either." Dawn gave Nancy another smile, then patted the strap of her backpack. "Well, I've got to get to the library. See you."

Nancy followed Dawn with her eyes until she disappeared through Thayer's chrome-and-glass doors. It hadn't exactly been a heart-to-heart. But at least there was hope that things could be normal between them.

Right?

When Nancy opened the door to her room a few minutes later, Kara was sitting at her desk, with her back to Nancy. "Hi," Nancy said, but Kara didn't turn around.

"Look, I hate all this tension between us," she said, going over to her roommate. "Isn't there some way we can talk about this?"

As she stepped around to the side of the desk, Nancy saw that tears were streaming down Kara's face. "Hey," she said more gently. "What happened?"

Kara's eyes were red and swollen from crying. "It's V-Vic," she said. "He b-broke up with me!"

"What? But you seemed so close," Nancy said. "I'm sorry, Kara. I know how much you liked him."

"Give me a break!" Kara burst out angrily. "You've been trying to sabotage my relationship with Vic ever since Scooter's accident." She looked around uncomfortably.

You mean, ever since Vic broke Scooter's hand? Was that what Kara was trying to say? Or, rather, what she was trying *not* to say? "Kara, does this have anything to do with what we talked about yesterday?" Nancy asked as gently as possible. "About Scooter?"

Kara glanced uncertainly at Nancy, wiping her tear-stained cheeks with her hand. Then she turned to stare out the window. "Until about a week ago, everything was perfect," she began. "Vic made me feel so special. We told each other everything."

Nancy wasn't sure what to say, so she just nodded.

"But then Vic started acting so—" Kara frowned, as if she were replaying a bad dream in her mind. "He started being so secretive."

A week or so ago? That could easily have been when the plan was hatched to fix the big game with Brockton. "Did Vic ever say anything about hurting Scooter?" Nancy asked.

"I'm telling you, he wouldn't do that!" Kara burst out. In the next instant her whole body fell back against her desk chair and she whispered, "I don't think he would, anyway."

Nancy could see that it was hard for her to accept that Vic might not be the great guy she thought he was. But she needed more to go on. "You sound as if you have some doubts," Nancy said.

Kara took a deep breath and let it out slowly. "Vic left the Beta party the other night," she said. "I'm not exactly sure when, but it could have been when Scooter was attacked."

"Where did he go?" Nancy asked.

Kara shrugged. "He wouldn't tell me. That's what was killing me. Suddenly he didn't want to talk to me about *anything* anymore! And when I asked him about his car—you know, the dent and everything? He said someone must have hit him, but he did act nervous about it."

She took another deep breath before going on. "I can't believe I'm even saying this, but I think he was lying."

The evidence seemed to be piling up that Vic was Scooter's attacker. But was he the mastermind behind the game fixing, too? And was he the one who was after Nancy at the lake? Nancy's gut feeling told her no.

"Do you know where Vic was last night, about eleven o'clock?" she asked Kara.

"That's easy," Kara said with a bitter laugh. "He was with me, avoiding all my questions about Scooter. He was so defensive. I don't know why he didn't just break up with me then. Why did he have to wait until this afternoon?"

"Why do guys do anything?" Nancy asked, rolling her eyes. Kara had at least cleared up one thing.

"If it's any consolation, I'm pretty sure someone else convinced Vic to hurt Scooter," Nancy said. "If he did it," she added hurriedly. "Did you ever see him with anyone who seemed suspicious? Or hear him talking about Scooter or about throwing the game with Brockton? Any comment that didn't make sense to you?"

Kara thought for a moment, then shook her head. "It's not like we're Siamese twins or anything. I didn't see him every second. Mostly just with his buddies at Beta. Things always seemed normal. Then again, I'm not a very suspicious person," she said. "I feel like such a fool. I thought Vic really loved me."

"Maybe he does," Nancy told her. "That could be why he broke up with you. He couldn't keep up an act around someone he cares about, but he couldn't risk getting caught, either, even for you."

"You think?" Kara asked hopefully.

"Definitely." As Nancy thought about it, an idea came to her. It was a long shot.

"Kara, would you be willing to talk to Vic again?" she asked.

Kara stared at her as if she'd lost her mind. "He just rejected me," Kara said. "Right now Vic Margolis is the last person I want to talk to."

"It could be important," Nancy urged. "He'll be more likely to open up to you than to anyone else. If you tell him everything that we've figured out and threaten to go to campus security, that might scare him into giving you the name of whoever's in charge of this."

"I bugged him plenty yesterday and today, and he didn't admit anything. Why would he now?" Kara asked, but Nancy could tell that she was thinking the idea over.

"If he knows he's going to get caught, he could help himself by helping us catch the guy."

Kara took a deep breath, then gave Nancy a shaky smile. "Okay," she agreed. "I'd better call him now, before I lose my nerve."

"Tom Bowles called. Can't meet you tomorrow morning. Will call again to reschedule."

Leslie frowned at the note that was scrawled on the message board hanging on the door to her and Bess's room. So many details were missing: Why couldn't Tom meet her? When would he call to reschedule? Why did he call the phone in the lounge instead of her private line? Was he avoiding her?

It wasn't that she was angry. Just thorough. And his message was so incomplete. It was natural that she'd feel dissatisfied.

Going into her room, Leslie saw that the answering machine hooked up to their private phone was blinking. Maybe Tom had called to explain, she thought hopefully. Actually, it was thoughtful of him to respect her privacy that way.

"Beep! Hi, Bess, it's Brian. We have to talk—"

Leslie groaned and fast-forwarded the tape. "Beep! Come on, Bess, pick up!" Brian again. Rolling her eyes, Leslie forwarded to the next message, but that one was from Brian, too. When she got to the end of the tape, she couldn't believe it. All eight messages were from Brian. What was his problem?

Just then the door banged open and Bess came racing in. She dropped a pile of books on her desk, then collapsed on her bed and threw her arms over her face. "My life is over!" she wailed.

Why did Bess always have to be so melodramatic about every little thing in her life? "What happened? Did you break a nail?" Leslie asked. "By the way, Brian called. Eight times."

Bess lifted her arm and stared at Leslie in horror. "I can't talk to him. If he calls again, tell him I'm not here."

"I wish you'd talk to your friends about not using up the tape on the answering machine with long messages," Leslie replied sternly. "I was expecting to hear from Tom about something important." She gave Bess a dismissive look before adding, "Not that you'd consider studying important."

Suddenly Bess blinked. "That's it!" she said, sitting bolt upright. "That's how I can avoid Brian."

She rummaged frantically in her shoulder bag, then pulled out a scrap of paper with a phone number on it. "Here it is," Bess murmured. She reached for the phone. "Hello, Tom?"

"Tom?" Leslie echoed automatically. "Tom Bowles?"

Bess nodded distractedly, then spoke into the receiver. "I was wondering if your offer to help me with bio still stands? . . . What? . . . Tomorrow morning sounds good. . . . Ten-thirty? . . . Okay."

Leslie's mouth fell open. Ten-thirty tomorrow

morning was exactly when she was supposed to meet with Tom. So if he canceled on her, why was he suddenly free to help Bess?

As Bess babbled on, Leslie sat down at her desk. When it came to studying, Bess was a hopeless case. Even Tom wouldn't be able to help her catch up in biology. And when her poor grades came crashing down around her . . .

"You'd better not come to me for help," Leslie murmured.

I can't believe I'm actually resorting to studying, Bess thought a few minutes later. Is my life that bad?

In the last few hours her only chance for romance had evaporated into thin air and she'd completely blown the biggest dramatic opportunity she would ever have.

She could hardly bring herself to think about the audition. She'd been so upset about Brian that she didn't even remember what she'd said or done up there on the stage. But it was a pretty safe bet that she'd made a complete fool of herself.

Afterward she got out of there as fast as she could. She'd heard Brian calling her, but there was no way she could face him. Now, if she could just figure out how to avoid him for the next four years.

"I might as well die," Bess groaned. She flopped down on her bed and covered her face with her pillow.

As if in a bad dream, she heard the knock on the door, followed by Brian's voice calling, "Bess! Are you in there? I have to talk to you!"

Bess sat bolt upright, waving her hands frantically at Leslie. "Tell him I'm not here," she mouthed.

Leslie was already halfway to the door. Shooting Bess a smug smile, she opened the door and said calmly, "Hi, Brian. Bess is right here."

What did I ever do to you? Bess wanted to ask, but of course she couldn't. Not with Brian standing there, studying her with those big, worried green eyes. "Hi," she said, trying to compose herself.

"Bess, we need to talk."

The next thing she knew, he had grabbed her arm and pulled her into the hall. He didn't let go of her until they reached a remote window seat, set into one of Jamison's Gothic turrets, at the very end of the hall.

"Why are you doing this to me?" she asked. She stared at the tiny, diamond-shaped glass panes above the window seat. "Haven't I embarrassed myself enough already?"

"Bess, I want to apologize. Will you please look at me!"

Brian's voice was so imploring that she did. The expression on his face was troubled and concerned. It only made her feel worse.

"Look, you don't have to treat me like a charity case," she told him. "You found someone you care about, and I'm really happy for you. Now will you please leave me alone?"

"Not a chance. We have to straighten this out first."

"Why bother?" she said, rolling her eyes. "The situation seems pretty clear to me."

"Not as clear as you think," he mumbled under his breath. "Bess, I had no idea. I guess I misunderstood your feelings for me."

"Tell me something I don't already know," she mumbled.

"You don't have a clue, do you?" Brian grabbed her arm and turned her to face him. She was surprised at the intensity in his eyes. "Bess, if I were going to get romantic with any girl, believe me, it would be you," he said.

Bess blinked, trying to make sense of his words. "Then why? Who are you talking about?"

"What I'm trying to say is that"—Brian looked away for a second, then took her hands and said in a rush—"Bess, the person I'm interested in is a guy."

CHAPTER 13

Bess's jaw dropped open. "You're—gay?"

"Would you mind keeping your voice down?" Brian said. "This isn't exactly public information, you know."

Bess barely heard him. "You really are?" she asked again.

"Yes, Bess. I had to tell you," he said, measuring out the words. "I couldn't stand to think that you felt rejected by me, or I wouldn't have told you, at least not yet."

Thinking back, it all started to make sense. Why he'd been so secretive and mysterious. Why it had taken him so long to declare his feelings. Why she didn't feel giddy and goose-bumpy around him—because he was friend, not boyfriend, material.

Bess felt an incredible wave of relief wash over her. Throwing her arms around Brian, she cried, "That's great! I'm so happy for you, Brian. I mean, I guess I didn't really like you, either."

"Gee, thanks," Brian cut in sarcastically. "You really know how to make a guy feel special."

"You know what I mean," she said, punching him on the arm. "I've never been really good friends with a guy before." She shot him a sheepish look. "I guess I misinterpreted what was going on between us. The truth is, I feel much happier being just your friend."

Suddenly she was bursting with curiosity. "So?" she asked expectantly. "Who is he?"

She could hardly believe it, but Brian actually blushed. "Chris. Chris Vogel. He's in Drama 101 with me."

"You told me that part already," Bess said. "Does he feel the same way about you? How did you meet him?"

"Whoa, Bess. One question at a time. Our drama teacher paired us up to read some lines, and we really hit it off," Brian began. "He's interested in directing, not acting. I think he's going to be working as a production person on *Grease!* Anyway, we've been getting together to have coffee and stuff before class. He's let me know he feels the same way about me."

"This is so great," Bess bubbled. "Nancy and George are going to die when they find out."

Brian grabbed her arm. "You can't tell them! You can't tell anyone," he said urgently.

"Why not?"

"I'm not ready to let anyone know," he told her. "My family doesn't know about me, and I'm not sure how they'll take the news. I'm afraid it's going to hurt them."

Bess stared at him for a moment. She'd never kept anything so major from Nancy and George, but she understood how important it was to Brian. "I won't say a word," she promised.

Still, deep down, she knew that keeping his secret from her two best friends was going to be the hardest thing she'd ever done.

Will stared gloomily at the dead TV screen. It was three in the morning, but he couldn't sleep. Every time he closed his eyes, he pictured George standing in front of him, staring him down with her beautiful, angry brown eyes.

Over and over, he replayed her words in his mind: "Don't you think you're being just a little unfair? I could use the support of my friends right now. I could use the support of my friends..."

He'd turned on an old western, just to block out her image. But it wasn't working. Not at all. Every time the hotshot cowboy gunned down the bad guy, Will felt as if he personally had pulled the trigger with George as the target.

"With friends like me," Will groaned, dropping his head into his hands, "who needs enemies?"

"So, Nancy thinks this Vic might be the one who broke Scooter's hand?" Pam asked George.

George nodded. It was Tuesday morning, and she'd already showered and changed after crew practice. Now she was going to meet Nancy at Java Joe's. "Kara's going to talk to Vic this morning to see if she can get him to admit it," she explained. "Nancy and I want to be on hand in case anything happens."

"What about Bess?" Pam asked, as she piled some books into her shoulder bag. "Isn't she going?"

"She's got a study date," George answered. "And believe me, she needs it."

"Well, good luck," Pam told her. She reached over to give George a high five. "At least now you can stop pestering Jamal."

"Yeah," George said. Actually, she still thought that Jamal was lying about something, but she wasn't going to bring that up to Pam unless she had to. "Well, see you."

George left the room and headed for the stairs. She didn't want to get too hopeful about what might happen at the coffee bar. Still, it felt good to know that they were getting closer to learning the truth.

George took a deep breath as she pushed through Jamison's front door and stepped outside. It would be great when she could finally walk around without feeling like . . .

"Hi, George."

George stopped in her tracks. She'd been so lost in thought that she hadn't seen Will. He was leaning against the wall to the dorm with his hands in his jeans' pockets. There were circles under his eyes, as if he hadn't slept, and he was looking at her with a serious, almost haunted expression.

Ignoring her quickening heartbeat, George turned away from him and started walking faster down the path.

"Hey! Wait up, George," she heard him call, but she wasn't about to stick around so he could insult her again.

Suddenly he was standing directly in front of her, blocking her path. She was totally unprepared to be so close to him—to those mesmerizing eyes and the scent that was already so painfully familiar. "Do you mind? I have to be somewhere," George said stiffly.

"I'm trying to apologize here," Will burst out, grabbing her arm.

George wrenched her arm free, but something kept her from walking away. Crossing her arms over her chest, she looked him right in the eye. "Then say what you have to say."

"Look," he began, taking a deep breath, "I don't blame you for being mad. I should have been there for you. What people are saying, about you and Scooter, I know you'd never do that."

"You weren't acting like it," George said. "When you called to break our date, you were about as warm and understanding as a block of ice."

"Maybe that's because you lied to me and I was hurt!" Will shot back. "How could you date a goon like Scooter? I thought I meant something to you. I thought we were—" He let out his breath in an angry rush. "Forget it."

"What?" she asked. She couldn't believe that she was hearing him say everything she'd hoped for. Except that now things were so screwed up. Just looking at the pain on his angular face made George feel her heart would break. "I do care about you, Will," she said quietly. "I never meant for—"

"Wait," Will interrupted. "This is happening all wrong. I'm the one who's apologizing here. After what happened Saturday night, I didn't give you a chance to explain. It wasn't until you yelled at me that I realized what a jerk I was being."

"I don't really blame you," George said slowly. "I mean, everyone told me that I'd be crazy to turn down the chance to get to know an amazing athlete like Scooter. I was stupid to listen."

The corners of Will's mouth tugged up into a smile. "Is that your way of saying that you'd rather be with a mere mortal like me than with a campus heartthrob like Scooter Berenson?"

"Trust me, the only thing about Scooter that's larger than life is his ego," George said. "That and his ability to drive like a total maniac while under the influence."

"You're kidding," Will said.

"I wish," George told him. "And just because I actually had the nerve not to fawn all over him . . ." She let her voice trail off. "You don't need to know the gruesome details. It's not your problem."

"That's where you're wrong," he said softly. "I want to help. Look, George, do you think there's any chance that we could . . ." He shook his head. "Never mind. I know you probably don't want to go out with me anymore. I just want you to know that I'm behind you a hundred percent. I'm going to tell everyone I know that there's no way you're the one who broke Scooter's hand."

Will gave her a long, searching look before leaning forward to kiss her on the cheek. Then he turned and walked away.

George's heart soared. Will believed in her after all! He really cared about her.

But deep down, she wondered. Was it too late for them to make a fresh start?

"Bio text, lab book, notes, calculator." Bess threw the items into her backpack, then zipped it up and grabbed her jacket.

No matter how much time she left herself to get ready in the morning, she always seemed to be running late. She was supposed to meet Tom downstairs at ten-thirty, and it was already twenty to eleven.

He's a friend of Leslie's, so he'll probably be very punctual, she thought as she hurried from the room. I just hope he won't hold it against me.

When she got to the lobby, Tom was there. He was reading the notices on the bulletin board, his backpack on the floor next to him.

"Hi!" Bess called out. "Sorry I'm late."

To her relief, he didn't seem too annoyed. "That's okay," he said, giving her a smile. "I don't have any classes until this afternoon. That'll give us a few hours in the library."

"Library?" Bess echoed. "I guess it's about time I got to know it."

Tom picked up his backpack and slung it over his shoulder. As they headed out the door, he said, "I dug up some old study sheets that might help you."

"I've already got dozens of those, and I can't make sense of any of them," she admitted. "I guess I should have warned you. I could be the ultimate tutoring challenge."

He shot her another mysterious smile, his eyes gleaming. "Then our study session ought to be very interesting—in more ways than one," he said.

What's happening here? Bess wondered. He wasn't exactly flirting, but there was definitely something going on with him.

"Maybe I should take a glance at those study sheets," she said to cover her curiosity.

"Sure."

Bess peered casually over his shoulder as he unzipped the backpack and rummaged around among his books.

Her eyes froze on a fuzzy red thing wedged in the bottom corner of Tom's pack, behind some books. Scooter Berenson's rabbit's foot! Hadn't Scooter sworn that his attacker had stolen it?

"Bess, you don't have to be afraid." Tom's voice cut into her thoughts.

Panic gripped her. What should she do? What should she say? "I d-don't?" she asked.

"Of course not," Tom said with an easy laugh. "Biology isn't the killer you think it is."

Bess laughed nervously. Could *Tom* be the person who'd attacked Scooter? It seemed crazy, but if she was right, she needed a plan—and fast.

CHAPTER 14

"Hi, Nan. Is Kara already here?" George looked around as she sat down at the table where Nancy was sitting, just outside the entrance to Java Joe's.

"Inside," Nancy answered. She nodded through the open door to the coffee bar. "Vic's here, too. They're talking."

George saw Kara and Vic at a corner table in the back. Nancy had chosen the table carefully, George could tell. From out here, they could keep an eye on the couple without being too conspicuous.

George signaled the waiter to bring her a cappuccino. "I shouldn't even drink any coffee. I'm already totally hyper," she admitted. "I just hope that Vic tells what he knows."

Nancy's eyes focused on something behind George. "What's Bess doing here? Isn't she supposed to be on a study date?"

Turning around, George saw Bess hurrying toward them, with Tom Bowles right behind her.

"Nancy! George! Boy, am I happy to see you!" Bess cried. She seemed so excited—manic, almost. It was pretty extreme, even for Bess. George had to shift her chair to get a look at Tom.

"Hi, Tom," she said, before turning back to Bess again. "What's up, Bess?"

"Aren't you two supposed to be in the library?" Nancy added.

"Yes, but I had to tell you the big news first. It's about Pinky," Bess said, grabbing George's arm. She was bouncing all over the place, looking at George and Nancy with frantic eyes. "You know, back in River Heights?"

"Pinky? You mean your ra—" George started to say *rabbit,* but Bess cut her off.

"Yes! My mom called to tell me that Pinky broke her *foot* in a car accident," she said urgently. "It was so bad, they were afraid they might have to amputate. Can you believe it? Her *foot!* That would be so awful."

George and Nancy just stared at each other. Why was Bess babbling about her pet rabbit? Pinky had died when they were still in grade school, but Bess was acting as if the rabbit had suddenly come back to life—as a person.

"I know, you're in shock," Bess went on, before George or Nancy could say anything. "I was, too."

"Well, that's too bad, Bess," George said, utterly perplexed.

Tom started acting restless. "Bess, we should get going."

Bess turned around and shot Tom a nervous glance. "Oh, sure. Just another minute." She turned back to the girls. "Well, I knew you guys would want to know, since we've been talking about *Pinky* so much lately."

Has Bess totally lost her mind? Pinky's name hadn't come up in years. But this really wasn't the time or place to get into it. "Yeah, well, thanks," George said. "See you, Bess."

"Okay." Bess gave them a final piercing look before she and Tom walked away. As the two left, George heard Tom say something about how sorry he was to hear about her friend's accident.

"What was that all about?" George asked, shaking her head in amazement. "I mean, how could a dead rabbit get into a car accident?"

"Beats me," Nancy answered, following Bess and Tom with her eyes. "Didn't you get the feeling that something was bothering her? But, why wouldn't she just talk about it? I mean, what was all that stuff about her rabbit? Didn't Pinky die when we were about ten?"

George nodded. "Leave it to Bess to pull out the weirdest information at the strangest times," she said. "If you ask me, the prospect of serious studying has sent her into a state of temporary insanity."

*　　*　　*

Nancy frowned as she watched Bess walk away. "Maybe we should have talked to her more. I hope nothing's wrong."

"Me, too. I didn't really know what to say, I was thinking about Vic too much," George said.

"Speaking of which, we'd better keep an eye on them," Nancy said. "Did you see? I finally got my jacket back from Kara." Not exactly the most earth-shattering news, but at least it helped distract them.

"What happened?" George asked. "Now that she's broken it in, she decided it's not good enough for her anymore?"

Nancy shrugged. "I don't care why she returned it, as long as I have it." She slid her hands over the smooth leather and slipped them into the pockets. Instead of the silky lining, her fingers hit something hard inside. "Hey, what's this?"

"Photos," George said, when Nancy pulled a stack of them out and held them up.

"These must be the pictures Kara took at the Beta party the other night," Nancy realized. Putting them down on the table, she and George started idly flipping through them.

Nancy chuckled at one shot of a group of students mugging for the camera. Another one showed Scooter and George.

"No, thanks," George said, picking it up and ripping it in half. "I have enough bad memories of that night without this."

"Well, if Kara has enough influence over Vic,"

Nancy said, "you might be able to put the whole thing behind you soon."

Suddenly something in one of the photographs caught her eye. She stared at the details more closely. "This is a shot of Vic in his car," she murmured, half to herself.

"Yeah?" George looked at it, then blinked in surprise. "Hey! There's a dent in his fender. Do you think Kara took this after he got back from attacking Scooter?"

"There's no way to prove that," Nancy said. "Look! He's not alone." She squinted at the person sitting in the passenger seat. It was a guy, mostly in shadow, but a ray of light lit up part of his face. "I could be wrong, but doesn't that look like Tom Bowles?"

George stared at the photo, then nodded. "It *is* him. I wonder what a science whiz like him was doing with a jock like Vic? Besides, didn't Tom tell us that he spent that whole night in the lab?"

Nancy's mind was churning a mile a minute. "He must have lied. I can't believe what I'm thinking." She looked again at the photograph, then gasped. "There it is! Scooter's lucky rabbit's foot. Vic is handing it to Tom," she said. She could just make out the outline of the lucky charm, and the photo had captured a glimmer of light reflecting off its gold chain. "Neither of them even seems to notice that Kara's taking their picture, they're so caught up in what they're doing."

"Wait a sec." George held up a hand, blinking. "You're moving too fast for me. Are you trying to say that Tom paid Vic to break Scooter's hand? That *he's* the game fixer?"

"Why else would Vic be handing over the charm?" Nancy said. "And why would Tom lie about being in the lab, unless he had something to hide? Kara never mentioned that Vic was friends with anyone besides his frat pals. If these two are hanging out together, I bet it's because Vic is doing Tom's dirty work. It all fits."

"Wow." For a moment George just sat there. Then she grabbed Nancy's arm and said, "Nancy, Bess is with Tom right now! No wonder she was acting so weird. All that talk about Pinky's broken foot."

"She must have found out somehow that Tom has Scooter's rabbit's foot," Nancy said, snapping her fingers. "That's what she was trying to tell us."

"I can't believe we didn't pick up on that," George groaned. "We have to do something!"

"Definitely," Nancy agreed. "But I don't know if the campus police will take us seriously if we just have this photo to go on." she said.

George jumped to her feet and grabbed the photo. "Let's show it to Vic. Maybe that will speed things up a little."

She strode into Java Joe's, with Nancy right behind her. Kara didn't look very happy to see them, and Vic looked even less happy.

"Nancy, didn't you say you were going to let

me handle this?" Kara asked, giving them a warning look.

"That was before George and I found this," Nancy said. Handing the photo to Vic, Nancy and George quickly told him and Kara all that they'd pieced together.

"You've got two choices, Vic," Nancy finished. "Talk to us now, or take your chances with campus police on your own *after* we tell them what we know."

For a moment she was afraid Vic wouldn't give in. He just stared at her and George with a stony expression.

"Vic, please," Kara pleaded. "If you care about me at all. If you care about yourself, tell the truth. That's the only way the campus police might go easier on you."

"I don't see Tom covering up for you," George added. "Why should you protect him?"

Vic stared down at the table. "It wasn't supposed to be like this," he finally said. "If Scooter had gone along with the plan to throw Saturday's game, none of this would have happened."

"You mean, Tom's plan?" Nancy asked. "He's the one who wants to fix the big game with Brockton, right? I mean, isn't he the person students go to when they want to gamble on sports?"

Vic shot her a surprised glance, then nodded. "He's been running a bookmaking operation," he explained. "I'm his go-between. I pick up people's bet money at a P.O. box in town and pay them when they win."

"Vic! How could you?" Kara cried, her eyes wet with tears. "How could you get involved with that? It's so sleazy."

"Tom fronted me some money for a bet, and I lost big," Vic answered miserably. "He said I could pay it off by working for him."

Nancy felt sorry for Kara. It had to hurt to learn all this about someone she loved. But they had to find out the truth. "You broke Scooter's hand, didn't you?" Nancy asked.

Vic took a deep breath and let it out slowly. "Yeah," he finally said. "I didn't want to. I mean, Scooter's a friend." He looked around desperately before adding quietly, "But Tom said that if I didn't— If I wouldn't throw the game myself— Well, you can imagine what he'd do."

"I bet he didn't have to twist your arm too hard," George said, crossing her arms over her chest. "You took a payoff from him, didn't you? You certainly had the cash to buy Kara a necklace. I bet you jumped at the chance to be starting quarterback."

"Look, I'm not proud of what I did," Vic burst out. "If there's something I can do to help make up for it, please, just tell me what it is."

"Actually, there is," Nancy told him. "You can come with George and me to the library right now. Our friend Bess is there with Tom. We think she might be in trouble."

"Should I come, too?" Kara asked worriedly.

Nancy shook her head. "We need you to call

the police and tell them everything," she said.
"Tell them to meet us at the library—fast!"

What am I going to do? Bess asked herself
again for the zillionth time since she'd spotted
Scooter's lucky rabbit's foot in Tom Bowles's
backpack.

Nancy and George obviously hadn't picked up
on her story about Pinky. Bess had known it was
a long shot, but she'd still hoped that they'd be
able to understand her crazy references to Scooter's rabbit's foot. They hadn't. So what was she
going to do?

Bess stared across the library study table at
Tom. He was pulling study sheets from his backpack and arranging them on the table as if everything was normal. The library was almost
deserted with only a few students at the far end
of the building.

Don't panic, she told herself. He doesn't even
know you saw it. But if you don't start breathing
like a normal person, he's going to figure out that
something's up.

"So tell me where you started to get lost," Tom
said.

Bess tried to stop hyperventilating. "Maybe we
should start at the very beginning," she said in a
tight voice.

"Good enough." Tom smiled at her, then
reached into his backpack. "I brought two calcu-
lators and—"

He broke off talking as Scooter's red rabbit's

foot tumbled out of the pack and onto the table. He quickly shoved it back into the pack, but his expression became guarded.

"You saw it, didn't you?" he asked quietly.

"Wh-what are you talking about?" Bess asked nervously. Tom's expression had grown cold. She started to get to her feet, but he reached out and latched on to her arm in a viselike grip.

"I knew it was just a matter of time before you found out. That was part of the challenge," he said in a voice that chilled her. "But I did think you were really something—cute, you know. Too bad this all had to happen. Now, don't think you can just walk out of here."

Bess winced as his grip tightened on her arm. "Actually, I was kind of hoping I could," she told him as she kicked him hard in the shin. Surprised and hurt, he released her arm for a second, and Bess ran. With Tom close on her heels, Bess headed for the front of the library.

She did a double take when she saw Nancy and George appear around the side of some bookcases up ahead. "That's enough, Tom," Nancy called.

"What?" Tom stopped behind Bess and stared at the two girls.

"The campus police are on the way," George added. "Vic told us everything. You might as well give up, Tom."

"Fat chance," he growled.

Shoving Bess toward Nancy and George, he took off in the other direction. But he was

stopped a second later when Vic shot from behind another shelf and stepped right in front of
him. Grabbing Tom's hand, he twisted it behind
his back.

"What are you doing!" Tom cried. He strug-
gled to break free, but he was no match for the
football player.

"Give it up, Bowles," Vic said. "We're ending
this craziness once and for all."

"Brockton scored again," Nancy groaned on
Saturday afternoon. She grimaced and stared
down the row of stadium seats at George, Bess,
Pam, and Jamal. They'd all decided to attend the
game against the Cougars, but it was hardly the
major sporting event everyone had been psyched
about.

"Some big game." Bess leaned forward in her
seat to look at Nancy. "The Norsemen are getting creamed."

"What do you expect?" George said. "After
all, Scooter is out of commission, and Vic is sus-
pended for the rest of the year. Without a first-
or second-string quarterback, we don't stand
much of a chance."

"I guess we should be happy," Nancy said. "I
mean, Tom Bowles is in jail, and George's reputation is intact again." She watched the kickoff,
then grimaced a few seconds later when the
Norsemen fumbled another play.

"I'm really glad for you, George," Pam spoke

up, squeezing George's arm. "Now you and Jamal are in the clear."

"You two are too much," Jamal said. "I mean, a guy can't even can't do a little moonlighting without you figuring him for a hired thug." He shook his head in amazement. "Women," he muttered, but his dark eyes sparkled with warmth when he turned them on Pam.

Nancy had to admit they'd been way off the mark about Jamal. Pam had told George about what Jamal really had been up to. On top of classes and his regular job at the sporting goods store, Jamal had taken on light construction jobs with a high-school friend who happened to be on the Brockton football team. The friend had been at Holliston Stadium to check out the competition, and when he saw Jamal he gave him his pay from their last job.

"I guess we were a little oversuspicious," Bess admitted.

"That's what Jamal gets for being so secretive," Pam teased.

"Hey, I was just trying to protect you," he said, holding up his hands defensively. "I knew you'd be upset if you found out I had another job."

"Hey, Nancy," a voice called from the aisle next to them. Turning, Nancy saw Gail Gardeski standing there. She was holding some typewritten sheets in her hand. "I thought you'd want to see this article. It's going to be front page center on this week's *Times.*"

Nancy glanced at the headline: "Junior Arrested in Game Fixing Scandal: Quarterback Maimed in Calculated Maneuver Off the Field."

She already knew what the article said. After all, she'd been working on it all week long with one of the paper's senior staffers. Gail had told her that as a junior writer she wouldn't get credit for the article, but Nancy didn't care. At least she'd proven that her theory about gambling wasn't just a trumped-up excuse for clearing George's name.

"Did you notice the byline?" Gail asked.

Nancy's gaze flicked down to the writer's name, typed right beneath the headline: Gary Friedman and Nancy Drew. "Hey! I thought you said I couldn't have a byline!"

"I decided to make an exception," Gail said. "You did top-notch work getting the *facts* on this."

Nancy didn't miss the emphasis Gail placed on the word *facts*. It felt good to know that she'd earned some respect. "Thanks," she said.

As Gail left, Bess squeezed Nancy's arm. "Fantastic! It's about time good things started happening for you on the paper."

"Hi, everyone! Sorry I'm so late." Brian Daglian ran breathlessly up the aisle and took the seat Bess had saved for him. "I couldn't resist stopping by Hewlitt to see if the cast for *Grease!* had been posted."

"Don't remind me," Bess groaned. "After the way I botched that audition, I'm giving up acting."

Brian's face was brimming with excitement. "Well, you'll have to wait until after *Grease!* closes," he told her. "You're in the chorus."

Bess looked at him in shock. "What?"

"You got a part," he said again. "We both did!"

"Oh, my gosh!" Bess exclaimed. "But how?"

"You did great in your audition, Bess," Brian told her. "I didn't have a chance to tell you because, well, you know why. Anyway, you had such a spark on that stage. I knew you'd get a part."

Nancy gave Bess and Brian a funny look. Bess had sworn that they were just friends, but it was obvious that something was going on between them.

"Well, I guess the next few weeks are going to be exciting for all of us," George spoke up. "I get to have my normal life back, Nancy has her newspaper, and Bess and Brian have the musical."

"Not to mention sorority rushes for me," Bess added.

"You're still going to go through all that?" Brian asked. "Didn't you say the Kappas all hated you after you yelled at them about George?"

"Well, Holly said that most of the Kappas were impressed with the way I stuck up for George," Bess said, grinning. "Plus, after they found out what really happened, they felt bad about saying all that stuff."

Just then a loud groan rose from the crowd. Looking down at the field, Nancy saw that the Cougars had just intercepted the ball and were making a clear run for the end zone. "Not again," she moaned.

"Looks like a lot of other people are as disgusted as we are," Pam commented. "The stadium is already starting to empty out, and it's only the third quarter."

"Looks like one of your suitemates is bailing out, too, Nancy," George said. "Isn't that Stephanie?"

"The one who came on to Ned?" Bess asked. She frowned down at the stream of people heading for the exits.

Nancy had already spotted Stephanie just passing the concessions stand. "Actually, I've been talking to some of the other girls in my suite about that," she said with a secret smile. "They all agreed to help me get back at her for that and make sure her date with Peter never happens tonight."

When Nancy got back to Thayer Hall, the first thing she did was check the clock hanging in the lounge. Good, she thought. Reva had set the clock back an hour, as she'd promised. The real time was a quarter to seven, but the clock read a quarter to six.

Nancy turned as the bathroom door pushed open and Stephanie hurried out. Her dark hair was soaking wet, and she was wearing only her green terry cloth robe.

"Why the rush?" Nancy asked, stepping out of the way as Stephanie raced past. "Running from a fire?"

"I never run from anything," Stephanie said smoothly. "And as for fires, things ought to start heating up after I meet Peter for my date."

Stephanie frowned as she looked at the clock. "Is that thing right?" she murmured. "I could have sworn it was later."

"Hi, everyone," Reva greeted them, coming out of her room. "It's almost six. Anyone ready to head to the dining room?"

"So that really is the time?" Stephanie asked, frowning.

"Sure." Eileen followed Reva from their room. She gave Nancy a wink, then asked, "Do you two want to come eat with us?"

Nancy nodded, but Stephanie completely ignored the question. "Peter's not picking me up until seven. I've got plenty of time to get ready," she said. As she started down the hall to her room, Nancy stopped her.

"Hey, I've got the perfect thing—a new facial mask," she said. "Skin Sensations just came out with it. Why don't you try it?"

Stephanie hesitated, giving her a dubious look.

"I feel bad that we didn't get off to a very good start," Nancy said quickly. She flashed Stephanie her most sincere smile. "Call it a peace offering."

"Well, okay," Stephanie agreed.

Nancy flashed Reva and Eileen a smile as she ran to her room. A few moments later she came back into the lounge holding a plastic tube. The timing ought to be just about right. . . .

"Here, I'll put it on," she offered.

Stephanie looked a little surprised, but she didn't refuse. Sitting down on the lounge couch, she waited while Nancy applied the bright blue goop. "Look at that color," she said, grimacing. "How long do I have to leave it on?"

"Oh, not long," Nancy said mysteriously. Her eyes darted to the lounge clock just as the minute hand reached the twelve. Any second now . . .

Just then she heard the door to their suite bang open. "Is Stephanie around?" Peter called out.

Stephanie drew in her breath and jumped to her feet. "Peter! What are you doing here!" she cried, clutching at the neck of her robe.

"Don't we have a date?" As Peter sauntered into the lounge, Nancy saw his eyes light up with amusement.

"Oh, no!" Stephanie tried to cover her face with her hands. "I mean, yes! But you're not supposed to be here until seven!"

"Which happens to be the time right now," Peter said, checking his wristwatch. He leaned against the wall, giving Stephanie a blatant once-over. "You really know how to pull out all the stops to impress a guy," he teased. "You look exceptionally—blue tonight."

Stephanie's mouth dropped open but no sound

came out. This is a first, thought Nancy. I didn't think anything could silence Stephanie.

"Are you all right?" Nancy asked, trying not to laugh.

Stephanie took a few deep breaths, and then her eyes narrowed on Nancy. "Bravo," she said. "But I hope you don't think the match is over."

With that, she stormed down the hall and disappeared inside her room.

"She sounds serious," Peter said, his eyes sparkling. "Whatever you did, I hope it was worth it."

"Oh, it was," Nancy said. "It definitely was."

George stepped out the door of Jamison, slipped on her headband, and started her warmups. It would be dark soon, but after sitting in Holliston Stadium all afternoon, she really wanted to take a run.

"Feel like some company?"

Even before she looked up, she knew it was Will. He was walking up the path from the mall, wearing corduroys and a jean jacket. The smile on his face was tentative, but George couldn't help smiling back.

"You mean, you're actually willing to be seen with me?" she asked.

"I guess I deserve that," he said, grimacing. "Actually, I have some news for you."

She'd been hoping that there was a little more to it than that—that maybe he just wanted to see her. But, she reminded herself, it wasn't going to be so easy to go back to the way things were before. "What is it?" she asked.

"Remember your problems with the Selective Service?" he began.

"How could I forget?" she said with a groan. "The bank still hasn't unfrozen my student loan."

"Well"—Will gave her a mysterious smile—"I never told you this, but I have an uncle who works in Washington," he began.

"D.C.? Someone who has connections in the Selective Service?" she asked hopefully.

"Not exactly. But he has connections who have connections there," he told her. "Anyway, he pulled some strings, talked to some people, and"—he grinned—"it's all taken care of. The Selective Service finally believes you're a girl. You should be getting an official letter from them soon."

"You're kidding!" Without thinking, George threw herself into Will's arms. "How can I thank you?" she said into his shoulder.

Will hugged her tightly, then leaned back just enough to peer into her eyes. "I think you just did," he whispered.

Very gently, he brushed aside a curl that had escaped from her headband. Then, he covered her mouth in a long, lingering kiss.

Her lips were still tingling when they finally pulled apart. "So," she murmured. "I guess it's not too late to make a fresh start, after all."

NEXT IN NANCY DREW ON CAMPUS™:

Everybody's buzzing with the news: Casey Fontaine, star of the hit television series *The President's Daughter,* has enrolled at Wilder University, and she's moving into Nancy's suite at Thayer Hall. But while interviewing the actress for the campus newspaper, Nancy makes a shocking discovery: Casey fears for her life! Bess, meanwhile, is also feeling the pressure. For weeks she's known the ugly truth about a certain guy on campus—a secret she must now reveal, no matter the risk. And even though Nancy's relationship with premed student Peter Goodwin is starting to send off sparks, she's finding that the line between love and danger can be razor thin... in *Don't Look Back,* Nancy Drew on Campus #3.